W. S. (Walter Shelley) Phillips

Totem Tales

Indian Stories Indian Told, Gathered n the Pac fic Northwest

W. S. (Walter Shelley) Phillips

Totem Tales
Indian Stories Indian Told, Gathered in the Pacific Northwest

ISBN/EAN: 9783337089719

Printed in Europe, USA, Canada, Australia, Japan

Cover: Foto ©Andreas Hilbeck / pixelio.de

More available books at **www.hansebooks.com**

Indian Stories Indian Told

Gathered in the Pacific Northwest

BY

W. S. Phillips

———

FULLY ILLUSTRATED BY THE AUTHOR.

———

CHICAGO:
STAR PUBLISHING CO.
1896

DEDICATION.

There are two wee tots of few summers not far from where I write who have listened to the tales of the Talking Pine with silent interest and wonderment. Their eyes grow big, and bigger as they listen to the wonderful doings of the strange characters of which I write, and when the story is finished they climb up in my lap and two tiny heads covered with curls, that shine like the flecks of gold among the mountain river sands, nestle close to me and baby arms circle round my neck. They snuggle close to me, awed, half believing that it is all real, but so interested in the fairy folk that they want "just one more story," and I must not deny it.

May their baby sweetness never grow less, and may their "Tah-mah-na-wis" be always ready to protect them on their journey through the life allotted to mortals, which is, after all, only a grown-up arrangement of the Talking Pine tales, that they now love to hear and half believe.

iii

To these two, then—to little Laura, the one with the curls of gold, and to her baby brother, little Elden—this volume is lovingly dedicated, with the best wishes of THE AUTHOR.

PREFACE.

The stories contained in this little volume under the title of "Totem Tales" are the result of careful study and research among various tribes of Indians of the Northwestern Pacific Coast.

The Indian peculiarity of narration is kept as nearly as possible, consistent with an understandable translation from the native tongue into English.

The Indian names are all spelled phonetically, necessarily, so they should be pronounced as they are written—by the sounds represented. The stories constitute the embodiment of the Indian mytho-religious beliefs, and, as they are gathered from several tribes, they will sometimes clash as to the doings or looks of some of the characters, and in some cases the same character is mentioned by a different name, arising from the different tribal languages.

The general idea of the white people seems to be that Indians believe in one supreme being, or "Great Spirit," which corresponds to the God of our Bible.

This is not the case at all, for their religion is a

mixture of Tah-mah-na-wis, or magic; Skal-lal-a-toots, or fairies, and Too-muck, or devils, the evil spirits, coupled with a vast legendary lore of a purely mythical nature—fairy stories, in fact—of which "Totem Tales" constitute a part.

They are a very superstitious people and have signs, charms, and incantations for everything. Magic plays an important part in every Indian's everyday life and is interwoven with his doings and those of his ancestors and of the magic personages described in the legends, as, for example, "Spe-ow."

Some of the stories contained in this volume were told to the author by the side of the campfire in the great forest of the far Northwest, others were obtained from "squaw men" who had married into the tribe and were familiar with the tales, others were gathered from men of long residence in the Northwest, who had heard them from the old Indian story-tellers, characters who are fast vanishing with civilization.

Cold type utterly fails to reveal the interest and fascination of these weird and simple tales as heard from the lips of some old and wrinkled member of the tribe, a trained story-teller, while crouched by the side of a blaze in the open air.

His eyes shine with interest in his own story, and he

acts as much of it as he can, posturing, gesticulating, talking with his hands as much as with his mouth, and the musical gutturals of the Indian tongue adding greatly to the story value of the tale.

The giant pines rise up and up from the circle of the light until they are lost in the blackness that is only intensified by the blaze. The shadows flit about as the fire flickers, and it is not long until every Indian in the circle of listeners imagines he can see demons and fairies in the nooks of every bush and peeping from behind the giant trees, and they are in precisely the same state of mind that children are who listen to, an l believe, the frightful ghost stories told them by some old woman.

It is another phase of voo-dooism, a dealing in magic and magic personages, and every legend has been called into being by the thirst of the human mind to know the origin of things which it does not comprehend.

The legends account for the presence of mountains and other natural objects, the beginning, or creation, of animals, birds, etc., and the reason for the world being as it is to-day.

At this late date it is difficult to separate the Bible stories told by missionaries, years ago, to the Indians, and which have since drifted into legendary lore twisted to fit the Indian view, and worn almost unrecognizable by many repetitions, from that part which is purely legendary and of Indian origin.

This the author has endeavored to do, using time and patience, listening to the same story from different sources, until the Totem Tales embody the pure Indian stories which are told around the winter night story-fire in the lodges of the Northwest.

With these words of explanation I launch these "Talking Pine" tales on the troubled sea of public opinion, with the hope that they will as greatly interest the young readers into whose hands they may chance to fall as they interested a group of little folks in one of our Western cities the first time I told them of "Spe-ow" and had to go away leaving them dancing on the lawn and calling, "More! more! tell us more."

W. S. P.

CREDIT MENTION.

For efficient aid in procuring the material for "Totem Tales" I am indebted to Mr. J. A. Costello, of Seattle, Wash., a fellow "crank on Indians" who tramped the great woods in company with me and jotted down the notes while my pencil was busy with sketches. Together we drew the stories, or many of them, from the people we met on this trip.

Mr. Ed. Grant, a personal friend and former resident of the Northwest, has also given me many inside points on the mysterious Kloo-Kwallie dance which have filled out my own knowledge of this ceremony. His graphic recitals of the everyday habits of the Quinault tribe have also helped to a truer insight of the wild men, and he got his knowledge from five years' residence with them.

Three of the stories, namely, "The Wind Dance," "The Rain Song," and "Kloo-Kwallie, the Medicine Dance," were first printed as they appear here in the

"Forest and Stream" of New York, and seemed to have had at least some interested readers; in fact, their comments started me on the idea of grouping these legends in book form.

THE AUTHOR.

CONTENTS.

ILLUSTRATIONS.

THE TALKING PINE

FAR away in the unmapped West, close to the edge of the last chain of hills that mark the rim of the land, is the Lake of the Mountains. The Lake of the Mountains is very deep and very blue, and it is pure and sweet, for it is cradled in the mountain valley, and the great peaks are painted in it, upside down, by the Skal-lal-a-toots, as they always paint things in the water.

To know the Lake of the Mountains is to love it for its beauty and its songs. The opal armoured trout and the bronzy bass are there and the burnished gleam of the lusty salmon is not strange to its waters.

All these things the Indians have known for many moons. They know that the blue woods which hover about shelter all kinds of wild things, so they have camped for many, many summers on the shore of the

19

Lake of the Mountains, and always at the same place,
which is on a point that puts out into the lake
and makes a sheltered cove with a sandy beach, where
the canoes can come against the shore, and where
the children may wade in the water.

Just back of the landing, on the top of the small

A SLOPING BEACH FOR THE CANOES TO COME AGAINST.

ridge of land that goes on and on up to the mountains, stands a great Pine, with a goodly space under
his spreading branches where a dance may be held
and a council fire be built. Back of this pine are other

pines, and back of them are others still, and others, until the world is blue with pines, and they cover the mountains even up to the deep snow.

These are only common pines, and the great one all alone, the one who is so very old and tall, and whose arms are withered in places, and whose head is grey

WHERE THE CHILDREN MAY WADE.

with age, is the Talking Pine, the wise one of all the nation of Pine Trees, and is the friend of T'solo, the wanderer.

I am called "T'solo" the wanderer, and I have been in many lands, but the Talking Pine has told me

about stranger things and stranger men than I ever
saw, and many nights I have crossed the Lake of the

Mountains in my canoe, that I might sit
at the foot of the great tree and hear the
tales. .

These tales I will now give to you as
I heard them, for they are good things to
know, and there is much of the wisdom
of age in them, for the Talking Pine is
very, very old, and very wise, and T'solo's
word is the word of the pine.

All the rest of the Pines are of the
nation of the Talking Pine, but he is the

The Talking Pine.

Tyee, the great chief of the tribe, and is the leader in
all the dances and songs of the woods, and the friend
of all the wild things that live in the woods. His wisdom is deep, for he is old and
has heard many councils, and
many councils make one very
wise. Because he is so wise all
things ask aid and good words
of him.

T'solo on the Lake.

Once there were many strange
beings in this country, and many strange things happened, so now there are many stories to be told to

those who do not know of these things that happened long ago. Now, all who love tales of the wild things, and of their wisdom, should come to the story fire; for while it burns will be talked the talk of the Pine, and there is wisdom and strange things to be told.

We will light the story fire and put a coal against the chinoos that is in the pipe, and when the smoke begins to warm the mind, and the fire begins to warm the bones, we will hear the tales, and through these tales you will learn the wisdom and of the good heart of the Talking Pine, the Wise One, that dwells by the Lake of the Mountains, which are piled against the great water by T'set-se-la-litz, the country of the Sun-down.

SONG OF THE WATERS

W HEN the story fire was burning the first time I came to listen to the Talking Pine he told me of the Song of the Waters this way:

"T'solo, the wanderer, listen to the tale of the waters.

"In the country called T'set-se-la-litz, which is the land of the Sundown, there is a great high mountain which is named T'ko-mah, the one that feeds.

"This is because the rivers that come from there are white like milk, and the mountain is white and round like the breast of a woman, and the people of the mountain give it this name because a woman feeds her children from her breast, as T'ko-mah feeds its children, which are the rivers.

"One river that comes from T'ko-mah is called D'wampsh, the crooked one that sings, and it tells tales of the mountains and of the woods to those who know its speech.

"Now Wee-wye-kee, the grandmother, is very old, and is a friend of the crooked one that sings, and is also my friend.

"Wee-wye-kee knows the language of D'wampsh and knows all his songs, and she told the songs to me,

T'SOLO AND THE TALKING PINE.

and now I sing them for you, T'solo. It is the song of the waters like this:

"I am the wild one, the crooked one that sings, D'wampsh. My father is the snow and my mother is

T'ko-mah. The heart of my father is cold, but the heart of my mother is warm, for it is the fire, and I am born. A-a-ah-na! And I am born!

Wee-wye-kee.

"I sing, I leap, I run— I, D'wampsh, the crooked one—and I am happy, for I know many friends. I know T'kope-mowitch, the white goat, that lives by my mother, and to him and his brothers, the mountain sheep, I have given many drinks.

Al-ki-cheek Shells.

"I know Mowitch, the deer, and Moos-moos, the great elk, whose horns are like the arms of a pine.

"I know Yelth, who is the Raven, the maker of

Mowitch, the Deer.

T'zum-pish, the Trout.

the fire, and I am at war with the fire. Ah-e-e-e! I am always at war with the fire.

THE ROCKS TRY TO HOLD ME. 27

"I love the woods, who are wise, and I love the ferns, who are small, and who shade my face with their fingers, and I love the rocks who are big, and strong, and hard.

"The rocks play with me and try to hold me with their big, hard fingers, but they can't! They can't! Ha! Ha! They can't! I run, I leap, and I sing, and

THE MOUNTAIN SHEEP.

I am free! I, D'wampsh, the crooked one, I sing and I am free.

"Ah-e-e-e, Wee-wye-ke, the grandmother, they can't stop me, for I am always going to the council of the great water that is by Ill-a-hee Al-ki, the land of the Bye and Bye.

"Come with me, Wee-wye-ke, come in your canim, and I will carry you to Ill-a-hee Al-ki, and give you Al-ki-cheek, the shells to wear in your ears, and to trim moccasins with. Ah-e-e-e, Wee-wye-ke, come and you shall have Al-ki-cheek, plenty of it.

THE FERNS AND POOL.

"I have got the gold that my mother gives me, ha! ha! The yellow gold that Squintum, the white man, seeks!

"Yes, I have it, plenty! plenty! plenty! But I bury

TO THEM I HAVE GIVEN MANY DRINKS.

it in my sand, he! he! I bury it in my sand, deep
down, and then I roar, and foam, and sing, and the
Squintum cannot find the gold, and it is well.

"Ah-e-e-e, Wee-wye-ke, it is well, for the white man,
Squintum, is thirsty to kill when his eyes shine with
the yellow gold. So I hide it and sing on, and let him
hunt!

"I sing to the rushes until they sleep, and I give
them drink for their thirsty stems. The willows, too,
drink of my water, and it is well.

"T'zum, the spotted trout, lives in my shadow and
waits until his grandmother, the Chinook salmon,
comes from the sea, the council of water, then he
grows fat on eggs, Ah-e-e-e, Wee-wye-ke, then the can-
nibal grows fat on eggs.

"I know Ena, the beaver, and Kula-kula, the wild
duck, and I know Enapoo, the muskrat, the lazy one
that sits in the sun. I know many, many more, Wee-
wye-ke, many more, and they are all my friends. Have
you not heard the song of the lonesome one, Wah-
wah-hoo, the frog? Wah-wah-hoo is my friend, too,
and sings at night for Hah-hah, who was his wife, and
who is dead.

"Now, Wee-wye-ke, I must hurry, for I hear the
song of the Skamson, the Thunderbird, and soon the

rain will come, and I must dance then and carry it to the sea; Klook-wah, Wee-wye-ke."

And so ended the song of the water as Ka-ki-i-sil-mah, the Talking Pine, spoke it a long time ago.

"COME, T'solo, the wanderer, when the wind is strong in the Southwest, and see the wind dance and hear the wind song of the pines." So said my friend, the Talking Pine, when we parted the last time.

This Wise Pine, which is so old that it can remember the coming of the first white man, had promised to tell me the secrets of the woods, and this was to be the beginning. So when the wind came from the Southwest I got into my canoe and journeyed across the Lake of the Mountains until I came to the place where the Wise One lives.

The Talking Pine and all his large family and all their relations were dancing the wind dance and singing the wind song when the canoe scraped on the sand.

The Talking Pine saw me and nodded his head, but did not stop dancing, for you must know that when the pines begin dancing they will sing and dance the wind dance just as long as they can get the wind to help them with the music.

They love to swing and to sway with the wind that comes from the sea to help them sing, and you know the pines cannot sing alone and they always sleep when the wind goes away.

I came to the foot of the Talking Pine so he could talk as he danced, and he told me why the pines dance the wind dance, and sing always when the wind is in the Southwest.

This the Talking Pine said about the wind dance:

"Many, many years ago, before I was born, or my father, or my father's father was born, when the wind was still a little boy, there were many strange and horrible creatures in the world, and they were always at war.

"Far away to the Southwest lived an old Skall-lal-a-toot that the wind loved to play tricks on.

"This Skall-lal-a-toot had a daughter about the same age as the wind, and the wind loved the little one for her winning ways and pretty face, for, you know, they are all this way.

"The old Skall-lal-a-toot loved his daughter very much, too, and hated the wind because he was always traveling and playing tricks, and had a bad temper.

"When the wind got old enough to marry he went to this girl and wanted her to go away with him to his lodge.

"She was willing, but the old Skall-lal-a-toot was very angry and hid his daughter.

SKALL-LAL-A-TOOTS.

"Now, you know the wind can make himself very small and invisible, so he came in the night and took the Skall-lal-a-toot's daughter in his arms and started away across the big water to take her to his lodge.

"Soon the old Skall-lal-a-toot missed his daughter and went to find the wind and get his daughter back, and at the same time to punish the wind for the trick he had played on him.

"After a long journey he overtook the wind, and while the wind slept he took his daughter and then struck the wind so hard on the head that he was like a dead man for a long time.

"Then the old Skall-lal-a-toot took his daughter and started for home again.

"When the wind woke up he was pelton in his head—crazy, the white men call it—and could not remember anything, and had lost the power to change himself back to his visible shape again, so now you can only hear him sing, but can never see him.

Moccasin.

"After a long time the wind remembered that the Skall-lal-a-toot's daughter was with him, and he thought she had been stolen, so he went to look for her.

"The wind was very strong in his body, because he was wrong in his head, and he traveled very fast and got very angry when he thought of the old Skall-lal-a-toot, and at last he overtook the old man with his daughter and fought him a great battle away out over the big water.

"Soon the old Skall-lal-a-toot was forced to drop his daughter and take care of himself, and when the father let go of her the girl fell down into the water and was drowned.

"Then the Tah-mah-na-wis took her up in the sky, so the wind could see her always.

"The white men call her the Moon, but they do not know why her face is white like the face of a drowned person, or why you can always see the ghost of the moon in the water when you look, on a moonlight night.

"That is because she was drowned in the big water, and now she must always stay there until the wind finds her, and the wind is crazy and does not know her face, but travels always and looks for his wife and sings to call her from the woods.

"The wind thinks the pines know where his wife is, and he is always singing to them to tell him; then he gets crazy again and thinks she is with him, and he goes away laughing and singing.

"The wind loves to dance and to sing, and the pines always help the poor fellow, and he tells them many things that he sees in his travels.

"He is not always crazy, and then he moans and cries for his wife, and looks everywhere, but soon he gets crazy again and sings and shrieks, and rushes along looking for the old Skall-lal-a-toot.

"The Tah-mah-na-wis changed the wicked old Skall-lal-a-toot into the sun and put him in the sky, and now he is always running away from his daughter and she is always following him."

This the Talking Pine told me as he danced the wind dance and sung the wind song.

"I would sleep now, T'solo, the wanderer," said the Pine when the wind went away. "When there is more to tell you I will let you know by a message and you will come then, T'solo, the wanderer, and we will see more."

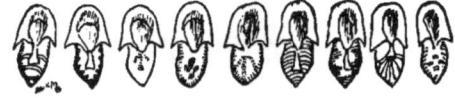

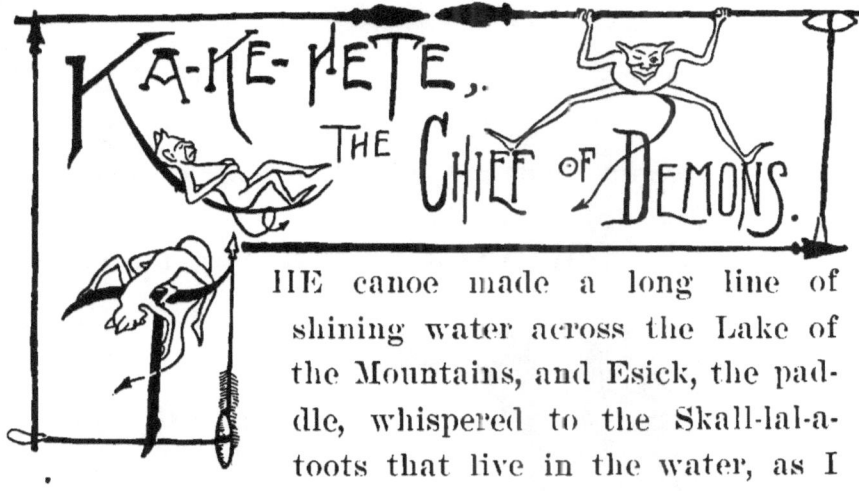

KA-KE-PETE, THE CHIEF OF DEMONS.

HE canoe made a long line of shining water across the Lake of the Mountains, and Esick, the paddle, whispered to the Skall-lal-a-toots that live in the water, as I went along toward the path that Snoqualm, the moon, puts on the still water.

You can never come up to this path because Snoqualm moves it away just as fast as the canoe travels, and he stops it when you stop, but he does not bring it nearer.

When the canoe came against the sand that is in front of where the Wise One stands it made no noise and I thought the great Pine was sleeping, he was so still, but he spoke and his voice was small like the voice of a man talking a long ways across the water, or a man talking in the night when Polikely Kula-kula, the owl, is flying, and he said, "T'solo, the wan-

41

derer, you are late to-night, and for that we can only have a short talk. There is a tale of Ka-ke-hete, chief of all the demons, that fits the night well, and we will have this, the tale of Ka-ke-hete."

"That is well, Wise One, for I would know of Ka-

THE NIGHT BIRD.

ke-hete, the chief of demons, so when I hear his whistle I may know what to do. Talk, and say the tale, Wisest of Pines."

Then the Pine began, and his voice was small and full of sleep.

THE PATH THAT SNOQUALM, THE MOON, MADE.

"A long time ago Ka-ke-hete, Chief of the Too-muck, was making a journey. For many days he trav-

eled in his canoe, and he journeyed with the water toward the council of waters, and this was on a river that is named Samumpsh.

"When he had traveled for as many days as the fingers of one hand and two more the wind saw him.

"By this time he was on the great water and there was no land close, so the wind, who is al-ways at war with Ka-ke-hete,

Ka-ke-hete.

sung a war song and ran over the water.

"Ka-ke-hete saw the wind coming and tried hard to reach the shore of an island, but Esick, the paddle, was slow, and the travel of the canoe was like the travel of a tired child, and so the wind caught Ka-ke-hete and fought him there in his canoe.

"Soon Ka-ke-hete fell out of the canoe and had to swim, and the wind thought he was dead of the water and went away singing.

Esick.

"Ka-ke-hete did not die, but swam to the island and hid there in the woods for a long time.

"When he saw any children playing in the sand
down by the water, then Ka-ke-hete ran down and carried them into the woods and ate them up.

"Now, this made the people very angry and very
sad, and they came together in a great council and

KA-KE-HETE ON THE RIVER.

said, 'This thing in the woods must be killed, so it
cannot eat our children,' so they went into the woods
to hunt and kill Ka-ke-hete, but they found only an
otter, for Ka-ke-hete had seen them coming and by
his magic had changed his form to that of an otter,

THE WIND FOUGHT KA-KE-HETE A GREAT BATTLE. 47

and so they did not kill him, for the people knew that an otter was not big enough to eat children.

"When the people all went back to their lodges Ka-ke-hete changed himself back to his own form, and at night went down to the beach and stole a canoe.

"With this canoe he paddled away from the island and went on his jour-ney, and so he got away.

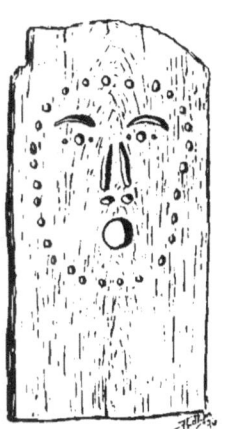

"Now you may hear his voice at night in the woods, and it is not the voice of Hoots, the brown bear, nor the voice of Itswoot, the black bear, nor the voice of Puss-puss, the cougar, nor the voice of Hootza, the wolf, but it

Carving of Ka-ke-hete.

Skal-lal-aye Mask.

sounds like all of these voices, and it sounds like the war song of the wind, but it is not any of these.

"It is like the voices of the dead people who are at Stickeen, the land of Shadows, and it makes you cold on your back, and your hair lay away from your head.

"It is the voice of Ka-ke-hete, the chief of the demons, who calls his tribe and sings for the little

Skall-lal-a-toots who live everywhere and who make much mischief.

"When you hear this sound at night, then drop your lodge curtain and see that the great Skall-lal-aye mask hangs on the lodge pole over your head, so that Ka-ke-hete will go by and not raise the lodge curtain.

"And this is the tale of Ka-ke-hete, the Tyee of all demons."

So said the Talking Pine.

"It was a good tale, Wise One, and I will hang up the mask in my lodge and drop the door curtain as I go in.

"I will come for more tales, and now Klook-wah."

And then I went with the canoe across the Lake of the Mountains.

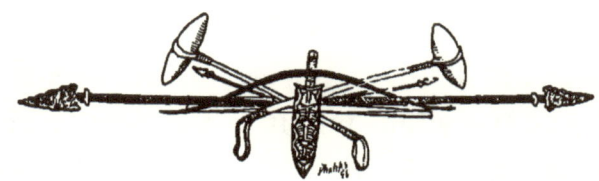

BIRTH OF SKAMSON

THE Talking Pine nodded in friendly greeting as I tied my canoe to the end of a log and let it drift on the placid water and mirror itself in the Lake of the Mountains, while I climbed up to sit at the foot of the Wise One and listen to the tales he had to tell.

"To-night we will know of the birth of the Thunderbird, Skamson, who makes the rain, T'solo," said the Pine as I lighted my pipe and waited at his feet, watching the moon rise.

"It is good," I answered; "I would know of the Thunderbird, Wise One, and how he came to be. Tell the tale and I will listen."

"Then it is this way," said the Talking Pine, and at once he began to tell the tale.

51

"Too-lux was the South wind, who always traveled North in the summer time.

"Quoots-hoi was an old witch who lived by a great river and whose home was by the rocks.

Too-lux.

"When Too-lux came to the river he was tired and hungry from his travel, and when he saw Quoots-hoi he said, 'Give me something to eat, for I am olo, hungry.'

"'I have nothing ready, but here is a net; go and catch a *little whale and bring it to me so I can cook it, and you shall have some fish for your hunger,' said Quoots-hoi.

"So Too-lux took the net, which was made of the small roots of the hemlock tree, and waded into the great water. There he soon caught a little whale and brought it to the lodge of Quoots-hoi and prepared to clean it to make it ready to eat.

"Then Quoots-hoi handed a knife, made from a sharp sea-shell, to Too-lux and said, 'Do not cut the little whale across his back, but split him along his backbone and dress him that way.'

Quoots-hoi.

*Grampus.

TOO-LUX CAUGHT A LITTLE WHALE. 53

"Now, Too-lux was very hungry and was in such a hurry for his dinner that he did not pay much attention to what Quoots-hoi, the witch, had told him, but cut the little whale across the back.

"When he did this the whale immediately changed and became a great bird, which flew away and lit on

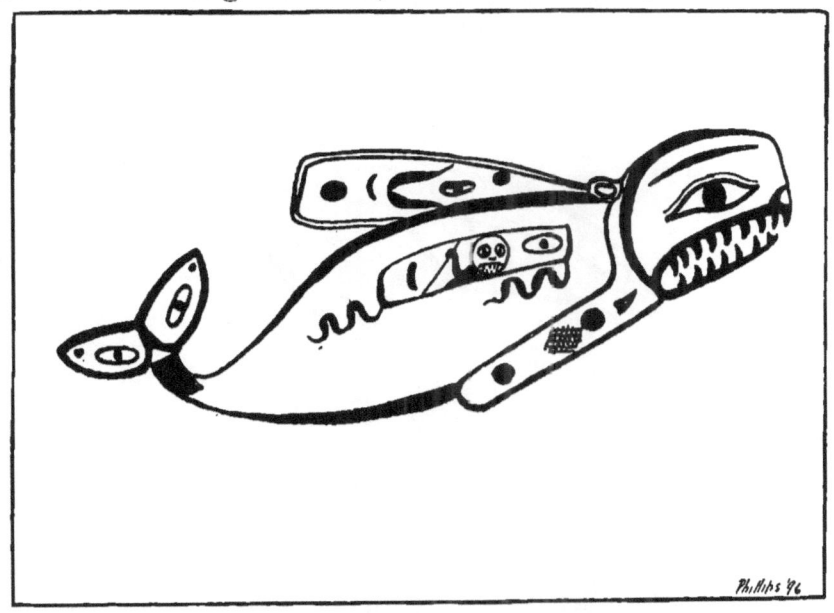

THE WHALE—HAIDA DRAWING.

a high mountain. There it built a nest and laid many eggs. Quoots-hoi and Too-lux followed the bird and found the nest. They destroyed all the eggs but one, and that one hatched before they could get around to break it, and so the Thunderbird was born.

"Before Quoots-hoi and Too-lux could capture and kill it the bird flew away and went to another high mountain and covered itself up with clouds, so no one can find it now, and it is the maker of the rain, and of Too-tah, the thunder.

THE LITTLE WHALE (GRAMPUS)—HAIDA INDIAN DRAWING.

"Some other time I will tell you what the Thunder-bird can do, and where he lives and what he eats, but not now, T'solo, the wanderer, for the moon is high and it is time to sleep. Come again and listen, for there are more tales to tell."

BUT TOO-LUX CUT THE WHALE ACROSS THE BACK.

And so I journeyed to my lodge again and left the Wise One to sleep out his sleep, for he is old, and those who are old must sleep much and are not like young folks, whose eyes are bright and whose feet are like the feet of a deer.

THE DEEDS OF YELTH

ELL me, Wise One, of the deeds of Yelth, the Raven," I said to the Talking Pine, as I came and sat by his feet.

"You would know of the deeds of the Black One, Yelth, the Raven?" he asked.

"Yes, Wise One, the story of the fire; tell me of this, and how it came about."

"Listen then, T'solo, the wanderer, for it is well to know of the fire, and how it came.

"Yelth, the Raven, is a good spirit and has done many deeds, so many that I cannot tell you of all of them. Nobody knows of all that Yelth has done, for he has lived a long, long time, and is always doing deeds.

"But of the fire: I know the tale and will tell of it and of the sun, the moon, the stars, and of the fresh

YELTH MADE LOVE TO THE EAGLE'S DAUGHTER. 61

water, which Yelth, the Raven, got from the eagle and gave to men.

"It is like this:

"When times were young and people did not have all the things in the world that they do now, the great

Yelth.

Gray Eagle was a mighty chief and was keeper of the fire, the sun, the moon, the stars, and the fresh water.

"He was the enemy of men and guarded all these things well that men did not get them for their own use.

"Now, Yelth was a friend to men and was always doing good deeds for them, and for this reason he was hated by the Eagle, who was his uncle.

"The Eagle had a pretty daughter, and Yelth made love to the girl, and so got into the lodge of his uncle, the Eagle, and looked

Ravens.

around to see what the Eagle had that would be good for the use of men.

"At this time the Raven was not a black bird, as he is now, but was a fine young man, who was changed by the magic of his enemies into the shape of a bird, and he was very wise himself in all the ways of magic, and so the Eagle's daughter loved him.

"Soon Yelth found the sun, the moon, the stars, the fire, and the fresh water, and he deserted his sweetheart and stole all these things from his uncle,

YELTH FLEW OUT OF THE SMOKE HOLE.

and, putting on his magic bird skin, flew out of the smoke hole in the lodge with them.

"As soon as he got outside he hung the sun up in the air, and putting on his magic bird skin again, soon reached an island in the great water, where he rested until it was night.

YELTH FLEW WITH THE FIRE.

"Now, when the darkness came he could not see how to travel, so he scattered the stars about in the sky and hung up the moon, so he could have light, and left them there for the use of men.

"When he found he could see to travel by this light he took the fresh water and the fire and started for his own lodge. Soon he dropped the water and it fell to the ground, and now there are lakes and rivers in the land, and men have good water to drink.

"With the fire he journeyed on, and soon all the stick burned up, and the smoke made his body black, and his bill burned until he had to drop the fire, and it fell in the rocks and in the trees, and it is still there, for you may get fire by rubbing two sticks together, and you may get it by striking two rocks together, too.

"And so that is the coming of fire. When you come again, T'solo, the wanderer, I will tell you more of the deeds of Yelth, but not now, so Klook-wah."

WEE-HAT-CHEE
THE RAINBOW

HE sun was painting the Western sky with bright patches of gold and rose when I lighted my pipe and got into my canoe to journey across the Lake of the Mountains and hold a talk with my friend, the Talking Pine.

The pisht, pisht, of the eddy loving paddle made sweet sounds and sung soft lullabys as I journeyed across the silent lake and looked down at the great mountains that are in the bottom, like silent gray ghosts, and in time I came to the beach of yellow sand which is just where the Wise One lives.

"Kla-how-ya, T'solo, the one who wanders," said the Pine, "it is a good night, a night of many colors in the sky, and to-morrow the rain will come, and then all the pines will sing the rain song and dance the rain dance, for the wise one, Skamson, the great Thun-

68

derbird, has sent me word, and he has said that Wee-
natchee, the Rainbow, will come with the rain to-
morrow.

"Know you, T'solo, wanderer, know you the tale of
Wee-natchee?"

LOOKED DOWN AT THE GREAT MOUNTAINS.

"No, Wise One," I answered, "I do not know the
tale of Wee-natchee, the Rainbow. Know you the
tale, Ka-ki-i-sil-mah, Wisest of Pines?"

"Yea, I know the tale. Light your pipe again, T'solo, for it is burned out and the smell of blue

Chinoos smoke is a good smell when tales are to be told. Make your pipe full of Chinoos, T'solo, and when the white man's fire stick makes the bowl red with fire and the smoke comes well, I will tell you the tale, T'solo."

Chee-chee-watah.

"It is well, and I listen, Wise One."

"Then it is this way," answered the Talking Pine.

"Siah-ah-ah Ahn-n-n-cutty, so long ago that I have no memory, T'solo, the wanderer, there was a great chief who was the head of many tribes and a wise man.

"This man's name was Chee-wat-um, the one who stays at home.

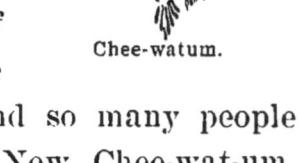

"He was wise in the ways of men and wise in the ways of the

Chee-watum.

Tah-mah-na-wis, and of magic, and so many people came to see him for his wisdom. Now, Chee-wat-um,

GAVE CHETIL A MAGIC BEAR SKIN. 71

the wise one, had a daughter who was fair and fresh
as the first white water flower of the lake that blos-
soms in the frog moon, and was wise in the ways of
men, for she was born with teeth, and as you know,
T'solo, she had lived before, else she would have been
born the same as other children—
without teeth.

"This girl was loved more than all
else by her father and was named by
him the Humming Bird, Chee-chee-
watah.

"Now, among others who came to
council with Che-wat-um was a young

White Water Flower.

warrior, who was Chethl, the Lightning, because of
his quick ways.

"When Chethl saw Chee-chee-watah he said in his
own thoughts, 'This girl shall be my wife, for she has
a fair face and much wisdom,' and so he set about to
make love to her.

"Chee-chee-watah, the Humming Bird, soon loved
Chethl, the Lightning, and they planned to marry and
live in a lodge of their own, and all was settled but
the word of Che-wat-um, her father. When he found
that his daughter loved the Lightning he was very
angry and put Chee-chee-watah in the woman's lodge

for many days, and sent Chethl away and told him never to see Chee-chee-watah again.

"Now, this made the young folks very sad, for they loved each other very dearly, and for many days Chethl planned to see the Humming Bird, but failed.

LEFT HER BODY LYING ON THE FLOOR.

"Then he thought of the ways of magic, and so went alone in the forest and called his great Tah-mah-na-wis to him and said, 'I, Chethl, the Lightning, am much in love with Chee-chee-watah, the daughter of Che-wat-um, the wise one who stays at home. Chee-chee-

watah is kept in the woman's lodge and I cannot see
her. Give me a charm that will make all eyes but the
eyes of the Humming Bird blind when I walk by them,
so I may go to her.'

"And so the Tah-mah-na-wis gave to Chethl a magic

MADE MAGIC MEDICINE.

bear skin and said, 'Put on this bear robe and go to
your sweetheart, for no eye may see you when you are
covered with it. But be careful that you look toward
the rising sun and toward the setting sun when you
put it on, or else it will lose its magic and be as other
bear robes, and of no use.'

"Then Chethl put on the robe and went to the woman's lodge, and no one saw him, and he said to Chee-chee-watah, the Humming Bird, 'Come under the robe and you shall go out of the sight of men, and we will go far away and live in a lodge of our own.'

"So Chee-chee-watah got under the robe and they went far away into the forest and built a lodge and lived there together until one day Chetl put on the magic robe, but forgot to look toward the rising sun and toward the setting sun, and then a strange thing happened. When the bear robe fell over the shoulder of Chetl there was a great noise and a strong wind, and Ka-ke-hete, the chief of the demons, came and took Chetl away and left Chee-chee-watah alone in the forest.

"When she waited for many days and Chetl did not come back Chee-

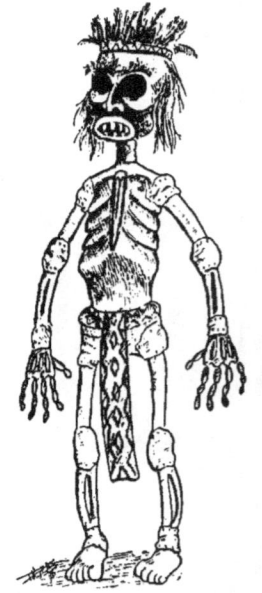

The Keeper of the Dead
—Indian Carving.

chee-watah was very sad and mourned all the time for her lost husband.

"Soon there came a time when Cole-sick, the keeper of the dead, came and found Chee-chee-watah sitting there mourning, and he took her away with him and

left only her body lying on the floor of the lodge, and
there she was found by her father, Che-wat-um, who
had been looking for her for many moons.

"When he found she was dead he was very sad,
and made magic medicine and so called her back from
the country of the shadows and made her to be the
rainbow, Wee-natchee, and put her in the sky, so he
could see her always, because she was dead and could
no longer be his daughter, Chee-chee-watah.

"And so this is how Wee-natchee, the Rainbow,
came in the sky.

"Now, T'solo, the wanderer, go in your canoe to
your lodge across the Lake of the Mountains, and
fasten the door curtain, for Ka-ke-hete, the chief of the
demons, is blowing his whistle and coming fast over
the woods and chasing the wind, so it is well for you
to be by the lodge fire when they pass by, that you
may not see his wicked face."

And so I crossed over the Lake and sat in my lodge
while Ka-ke-hete walked across the Lake of the Mountains and made the water white while it sung a war
song with the wind.

CAWK, THE BEAVERS' DAUGHTER

"NOW you of Cawk, the daughter of T'sing, the Beaver, T'solo?" asked the Talking Pine when next I sat at his feet and watched the little waves that always wash the sand and sing there in the Lake of the Mountains.

"No, Wise One, I do not know of Cawk, the daughter of T'sing, and I would hear the tale."

"Listen then, T'solo, the wanderer, for it is a tale that is good to know, for it shows how one can be too proud, and in this lose the good and get only the bad of living, and that is not a good thing to do.

"This is the tale, wanderer:

"Many, many summers ago there lived a chief who was T'sing, the Beaver, all alone on a great island in the big water.

"Now, T'sing, the Beaver, had a daughter who was

CAWK, THE BEAVER'S DAUGHTER, GOES WITH THE CHIEF OF THE SEA GULLS—HAIDA DRAWING.

Cawk, the one with the pretty face. Her mother had long been dead, and she lived there alone with her father, and so grew up to be a pretty girl, Cawk.

"All the young men of the country around came to make love to Cawk, the pretty one, but to all she was

T'SING, THE BEAVER.

the same, and was too proud to be any but the wife of a great chief, and so she waited.

"One time, when the ice melted and the water was unlocked, a great white bird who was T'kope Kula-Kula, the sea gull, came to the island where the Beaver, T'sing, lived, and saw Cawk, the pretty one.

"'Now the sea gull fell in love with Cawk and made love to her with his song this way:

"'Come with me! Come into the land of the birds where there is never hunger.

"'Where my lodge is made of the most beautiful woods, and where I, T'kope Kula-kula, am chief.

A LODGE OF FISH-SKINS.

"'Your fire shall always burn with wood.

"'You shall rest on soft bear robes.

"'My people, the gulls, shall bring your food.

"'Their feathers shall make your robes.

"'Your basket shall always be filled with meat.'

"So Cawk listened to the song and soon she loved T'kope Kula-kula, the sea gull, and went away with him across the big water, and lived in his lodge.

"Only too soon poor Cawk, the pretty one, found that she had made a mistake when she sent all the young men away and went with T'kope Kula-kula,

KILLED HIM AND CUT OFF HIS HEAD.

the chief of the sea gulls, for his lodge was not built of beautiful woods, but only of the skins of fishes, and was full of holes where Colesnass, the winter, came in and froze her fingers.

"Instead of soft bear robes, her bed was only the

skins of Tipsu Ko-shoo, the hair seal, the water pig, and she could not rest.

"And there was no wood for the lodge fire, and no meat in the basket, and the only food she had was the nasty fish that the tribe of the gulls threw to her, and that was not much of anything, for the gulls are always hungry and eat all they can get themselves.

"So Cawk, the daughter of T'sing, the Beaver, grew sad in her mind and longed for her old home with her father, and in her sadness she sung her song this way:

" 'T'sing, oh, my father, listen:

" 'If you knew how sad I am you would come to me.

" 'We would cross the big waters in your canim.

" 'The tribe of T'kope Kula-kula do not look on me with good hearts, for I am a stranger.

Tipsu Koshoo, the Seal.

" 'Colesnass blows his breath on me and Ka-ke-hete whistles by my bed.

" 'I have no food.

" 'I am sick and am very sad.

" 'Come, father, with your canim and take me home.'

"Now, when the summer came again T'sing got in his canoe and crossed the big waters to go on a visit to his daughter.

HE CUT HER FINGERS OFF.

"She was very glad to see him and begged him to take her home again, and told him how she had been treated by her husband, T'kope Kula-kula.

"When T'sing, the Beaver, heard of this he was very angry and waited until T'kope Kula-kula came back to the lodge and then T'sing killed him and cut off his head.

"Then he took Cawk, who was no longer the pretty one, because her eyes were red with tears, with him in his canoe, and went swiftly across the big water on his way home again.

"Soon the tribe of T'kope Kula-kula came home and found their chief dead, and his wife gone, and they all began to cry and they still cry to this day for their chief.

"All the tribe of gulls went in search of the killer of their chief, and soon they saw the canoe of T'sing, the Beaver, journeying across the big water.

"Then they stirred up a heavy storm, and made the water rise up in great waves that tried to sink the canoe of T'sing, the Beaver.

"When the storm came T'sing did a very wrong thing, for he took Cawk, his daughter, and threw her out in the big water for the birds to take revenge on.

"But Cawk caught the edge of the canoe, and held

on, until her father, to save himself, cruelly cut her
fingers off at the first joint. Now, the ends of her
fingers fell into the water, and the first one was
changed into the whale, and the finger nail became
the whalebone and so the whale came into the world.

CALLED TO HER TOTEM, HOOTZA.

"The second finger became a Grampus, or little
whale, and the others swam away in the shape of Salmon, Herring, Codfish, Seals, and Hairseals, and so
these things all came into the big water and are still
there.

"When Cawk fell into the big water the gulls thought she was dead of the water and went away, and so the waves calmed down, and her father took poor Cawk back into the canoe, and took her home, but she had no fingers and was in much pain.

"Now when she sat by her father's fire, and looked at her hands, all the love went out of her mind and Ka-ka-hete, the chief of the demons, came into it, because her father had been so cruel to her.

"So she counseled with Ka-ka-hete and he told her to make medicine to hurt her father.

"Then Cawk called to her Totem spirit, who was Hoot-za, the

Hootza, the Wolf.

wolf, and to him she said: 'My father, T'sing, the Beaver, has cut off my fingers. Bring all the tribe of Hoot-za and let them gnaw off the hands and feet of my father while he sleeps, so that Ka-ka-hete will go out of my mind, and I may sleep.'

"And so the tribe of Hootza came and gnawed off the hands and feet of T'sing, the Beaver, while he slept, and when he awoke he was very angry and talked with a bad tongue to his Tah-mah-na-wis, because he let Hootza eat his hands and feet.

"When he did this, the Sah-hale Tah-mah-na-wis was very angry, and made the ground open up in a great hole, and down went T'sing, the Beaver, Cawk, the pretty one, and all the tribe of Hootza, the wolf, except one, and from him came all the wolves in the world, and they are all bad, because of the bad deeds of Hootza."

This was the tale of Cawk, the daughter of T'sing, the Beaver, that the Wise One, Ka-ki-i-sil-mah, the Talking Pine, told me by the Lake of the Mountains.

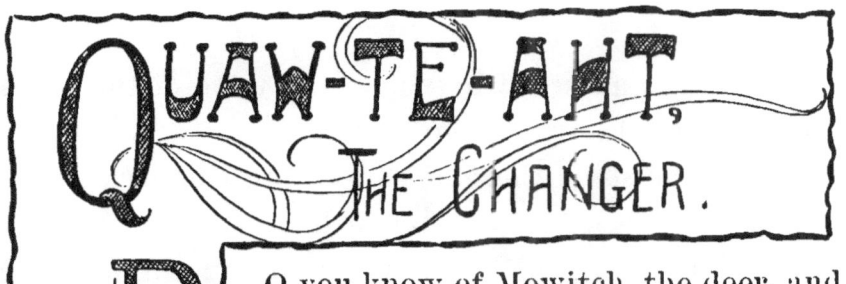

QUAW-TE-AHT, THE CHANGER.

D O you know of Mowitch, the deer, and how he came, T'solo, the wanderer?" asked the Talking Pine as the moon, Snoqualm, made a silver path across the Lake of the Mountains, from the black pines on the other side, clear up to the beach of yellow sand, where my canoe made a black spot on the water close by my foot.

"I listen for the tale, Wise One," I answered, and then watched Snoqualm, the moon, climb up the sky while the Talking Pine told me this tale:

"Mowitch was once a man, but is now a deer, be-cause of the magic of Quaw-te-aht, who did many other deeds, too, and it was this way," said the Pine.

"A long time ago Quaw-te-aht, the changer, came across the land and traveled along through the woods.

"In his travels he came to a place where the rain

91

was falling and stood by one of the tribe of the pines
to wait until the rain went away.

"While he stood there he saw a man who was stand-ing still and throwing his
hands about in the air over
his head very fast, and try-
ing to keep the rain from
falling on him in this way.

"When Quaw-te-aht saw
this he thought this man
was very foolish, and he said
to him, 'Why do you do
this?'

"'That is the way to keep
the rain from falling on
you,' said the man.

"'You are foolish, and for
your foolish ways, I will
change your form,' said
Quaw-te-aht, the changer.
'Go and be always in the

Quaw-te-aht.

form of Chee-chee-watah, the Humming Bird, and
throw your arms fast for the rest of your life.'

"And so by the magic of Quaw-te-aht the man was
changed into the form of the little bird that makes a

A LITTLE BOY CRYING.

noise with his wings, Chee-chee-watah, and now you will always see him when the rain has just gone, or when the tears of Snoqualm, the moon, fall at the coming of Polikely, the night, all because of his foolish ways when he was a man.

"Now, since this was done, no Indian is afraid of·the rain, and does not care if it falls on him, because he remembers the Humming Bird, Chee-chee-watah.

Chee-chee-watah.

"After the rain went away, Quaw-te-aht went on through the woods and came to a little boy who was sent by his mother to pick a basket of Shot-o-lilies, the Huckleberry, and this little boy was crying, 'Hoo! Hoo! Hoo!' because he was not a brave boy and was thinking of the Brown Bear, Hoots, who lived in the woods.

"So Quaw-te-aht said, 'Why do you cry?'

" 'Because I am afraid of Hoots, the Brown Bear, and think he will come and eat me,' answered the boy.

" 'Now because you are not a brave boy, and because

you cry always, I will change you from a boy to the form of a bird,' said Quaw-te-aht, the changer, and so by his magic the boy was changed into a dove, and is now in the woods and always crying, 'Hoo! Hoo! Hoo!' just as he did when he was a boy, and very much afraid of Hoots, the bear.

"So, if boys do not want to be changed into other things, it is best for them to be brave and not cry about Hoots, the bear, and then they will soon grow to be men, and be wise.

"Quaw-te-aht journeyed along and soon came to another man who was making sharp the edge of a stone knife, and to this man he said, 'Why do you make the knife sharp?'

" 'To cut meat,' answered the man.

" 'That is double talk, you make sharp the edge of Opitsah, the knife, that you may kill me, for I know your mind and can see your thoughts. Give me the knife,' said Quaw-te-aht, and started towards the man.

"Now the man knew that Quaw-te-aht saw his thoughts and so he was very much frightened and started to run away.

"In his great haste he dropped his knife, and then Quaw-te-aht picked it up and threw it at the man, and it struck him in the heel.

"When the knife stuck in his heel the man began to jump about and ran into the woods.

"Quaw-te-aht, to punish him for his evil thoughts, said, 'Go and be Mowitch, the deer, and jump about in the woods always,' and so by the great magic of Quaw-te-aht, the changer, this wicked man became

THREW HIS KNIFE AT THE MAN.

the first deer, and still jumps about in the woods with the knife in his heel, for you may see the handle of it sticking out just above the foot of the deer, where he has another toe, and his feet are split in two because the knife split the foot of the evil man.

"And so this is the tale of Mowitch, the deer, and
how he came."

When the tale was done, Snoqualm, the moon, had
climbed above the tops of the black pines across the
Lake of the Mountains, and was painting all the water
with light.

Then I got in the canoe and paddled away and the
voice of the Lake sung under the canoe as it went
along, and far away in the shadow of the trees I heard
the hunting cry of Puss-puss, the great yellow cougar,
who looked with his great green eyes for Mowitch, the
deer, for his meat, and from a dead pine, Polikely Kula-
kula, the big owl, sung for his wife to come, and so I
journeyed home to my lodge hearing these sounds.

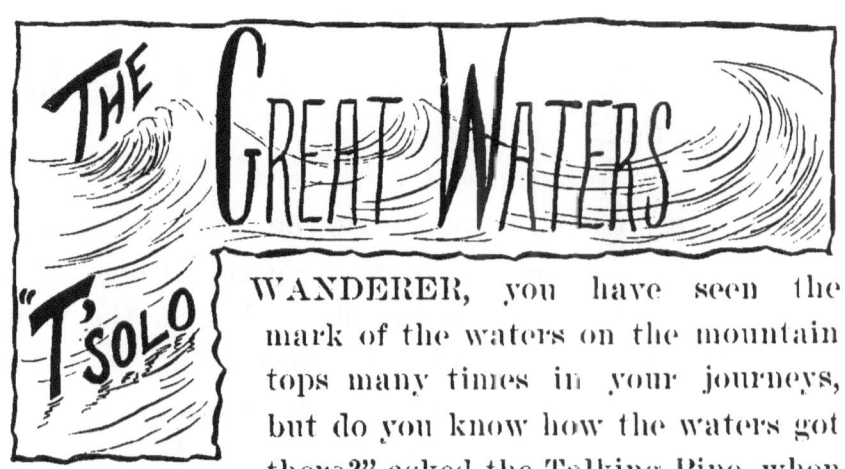

THE GREAT WATERS

"T'SOLO"

WANDERER, you have seen the mark of the waters on the mountain tops many times in your journeys, but do you know how the waters got there?" asked the Talking Pine, when I had sat down by his feet, and the smell of the Chinoos was in the air.

I thought heavy thoughts on this, but I could not think how the waters had left their marks on the top of the hills, yet I knew they had, for I had seen the sign in many lands, so I said, "No, Wise One, I do not know how the sign of the great waters came to be on the tops of the mountains, but it is good wisdom and well to know. Know you, wisest of Pines, how the waters came on the hills?"

"Yes, I know, T'solo, the wanderer, I know how this sign came there. Shall I tell the tale?"

99

"It is good to know of this, and I listen, Wise One. Speak the tale."

"Then it was because of this:

"A long time ago, before Yelth, the raven, was born, or before the coming of Hoots, the great brown bear, there were different men in the land from the men we know now, and they were not good men.

"Always they talked with a double tongue and knew much magic, but it was the magic of Too-muck, the evil spirits, and the magic of the little folks of the woods, the Skall-lal-a-toots, who are the makers of mischief and little bad deeds.

"All the men of the land were this way except one who was G'klobet, the silent one, and he was hul-loi-mie, different, and a wise man in the magic of the Tah-mah-na-wis.

"Now the men always counciled with the Tyee Too-muck, the chief of the demons, who is Ka-ke-hete, and who does many evil things, and they forgot the Tyee of all, the Sah-ha-le Tah-mah-na-wis, who is the spirit of good deeds, and who is wise and good to men.

"When the Sah-ha-le Tah-mah-na-wis saw these things, he was very angry and said, 'I will call Skam-son, the great thunderbird, and we will have rain and

MADE MAGIC TO CALL THE SAH-HA-LE TAH-MAH-NA-WIS. 101

the water will cover the land and kill these men who
are evil in their minds.'

"So then the Sah-ha-le Tah-mah-na-wis called Skamson, the thunderbird, and they held a council about
this deed, and when the council was done Skam-son
shook his wings and the rain came for many, many
days, and the rivers were full of water and
then overflowed.

"G'klobet, the silent one, saw these
things and he made magic medicine to call
the Sah-ha-le Tah-mah-na-wis, and then he
said, 'Why do the rivers rise while the rain
still falls? Soon there will be water on all
the land. What shall I do for meat?'

"Then the Sah-ha-le Tah-mah-na-wis said
this talk, 'Listen, G'klobet, the silent one.
These men are evil men and they forget the
Sah-ha-le Tah-mah-na-wis, the great Tyee,
and see only Ka-ke-hete, who is the chief of
evil deeds. Because of this, the thunderbird,
Skam-son, shakes his wings and the rain falls. Now
you who are G'klobet, the silent one, are not like these
men, for you call Sah-ha-le Tah-mah-na-wis, the chief
of all, and for this you shall be told what to do. Go
and get your largest canoe, and put all of your spears

A Salmon
Spear.

and nets in it. Put your mats and your bear robes,
and all your fine furs in, and plenty of meat and Kamas. Put your wife and all your children in, and leave
room for a rope of cedar bark that shall reach half as
far as a boy can walk in one sun. Then get in your
canoe and wait.'

"'The great water will rise and come up over the

MAKING CEDAR BARK ROPES.

land, and then it will come up to the top of the mountains. When it comes up to the top of the highest
mountain, then tie your rope to the highest rock and
wait again. The waters will come up over the top of

the highest mountain and up until you have no more
rope, and then it will stop and go back again until
there is no water but the rivers and the great water
as it is now. I have spoken.'

"And then the Sah-ha-le Tah-mah-na-wis went
away.

G'KLOBET LOADED HIS BIGGEST CANOE.

"So then G'klobet, the silent one, did all these
things that the Tah-mah-na-wis had told him and
waited, and still Skam-son, the thunderbird, shook his
wings for the rain to fall until it came to the top of the
mountain and then G'klobet tied his rope.

"When the other people saw what G'klobet, the silent one, was doing, they loaded their canoes and made cedar bark ropes, too, and when the water came to the top of the mountain they tied their ropes to the rock, too, and as the water came up they all let rope

THE OTHER CANOES DRIFTED AWAY.

out until they had no more left, and then the canoes broke loose and floated away, all but G'klobet, who had much rope, and whose canoe did not break loose, but staid there and came down by the top of the mountain, and so G'klobet got back to his home again when the waters went away.

"But the canoes that broke loose drifted away, and came down in other places, and so all the tribes of men came from these, and because they were scattered, and because they saw that Ka-ke-hete, the chief of the demons, could not stop the water from rising, they became better men and talked with Sah-ha-le Tah-mah-na-wis, and became wise.

"And so that was how the water left the sign on the mountain tops, and how the men came to be all over the land."

So said the Talking Pine, the Wise One, as I sat by his feet and watched the smoke of the Chinoos blow away with the wind, there by the Lake of the Mountains.

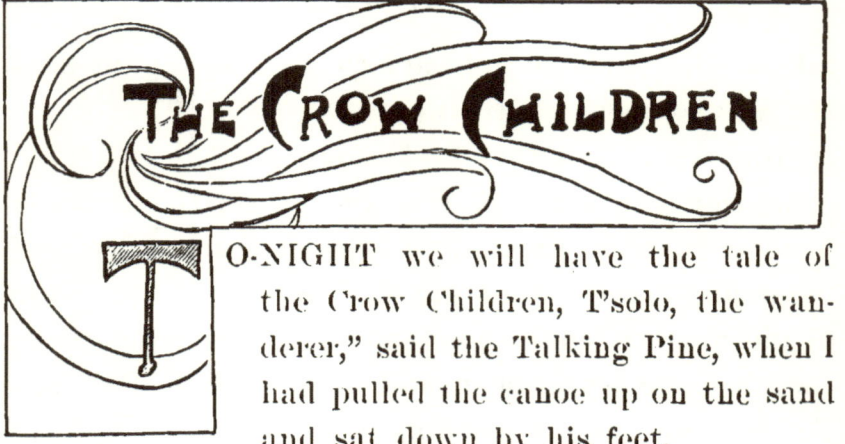

THE CROW CHILDREN

"TO-NIGHT we will have the tale of the Crow Children, T'solo, the wanderer," said the Talking Pine, when I had pulled the canoe up on the sand and sat down by his feet.

"Then I listen, Wise One," I answered.

"This is a story for children who do not mind their parents," said the Wise One, "and it is a warning to them to be good and listen to the voice of their elders, for who knows but they may all be changed to crows at some time, if they do not?

"The tale is like this:

"Once there was a woman who was the wife of a chief, and who had two children; she loved the children very much and always took them with her when she went away from the lodge.

THEY ANSWERED WITH THE VOICES OF CROWS.   109

"One time in the moon of the falling leaves she took them in the canim and went across the water to get some spruce boughs which the Indians use to collect salmon eggs on, as you know, T'solo.

"She pulled the canoe up on the sand and told the

LEFT THEM BY THE CANOE.

children to stay close by it while she went into the woods and cut the spruce boughs, and then she went away and left them there.

"When she came back both the children were gone, and had only left tracks in the sand up to the edge of

the woods. The mother followed into the woods, and
called them many, many times, and always they answered her with the voices of crows.

"Now the mother was very sad when she found they
were lost and she called her Tah-mah-na-wis to help

AND SO IT WAS HE CARVED THE TOTEM POLE.

her find them, but the Tah-mah-na-wis told her they
had walked into the woods, and that the Skall-lal-a-
toots had changed them into crows; that they must
always stay in the woods, and could not be changed

back into their proper form again because of the magic of the Skall-lal-a-toots, and so they were lost for all time.

"So then the mother went back and told her husband and wept many, many days, and the chief had

 the story carved in the great Totem pole in the front of the lodge, a n d there you will see it to-day,

The Crow.

and it is cut in all the totem poles of the Crow totem as a warning to all children not to disobey their parents, and it can be read there by all who can read carvings."

This was the story of the Crow children, and it is a good story to remember, for it is not good for children to disobey. When the Pine had finished I said "Klook-wah" to him and paddled away across the Lake of the Mountains to wait until another time.

KIT-SI-NA-O, THE STONE MOTHER

HEN I next saw the Wise One I had been on a long journey on the big water, and there on a lonely island away toward the home of Colesnass, the winter, I had looked upon Kit-si-nao, the Stone Mother, who sits in the side of the rock and weeps always. I did not know the story of this, though I knew it must be a story, for the mother would not be changed to stone for nothing, and have to stay there always, instead of going to the land of Shadows, and living there again, as all people do who have not done bad deeds.

So then I said to the Talking Pine, "Do you know the story of the stone woman, Kit-si-nao, who sits alone on the mountain, Wise One?"

"Yes, I know of Kit-si-nao, the one who weeps alone,"

SHE LAUGHED AT THE CHILD OF SKOOLT-KA.

said the Talking Pine. "Would you like to hear the story, T'solo, the wanderer?"

"Tell the story, Wise One. I listen."

"Then this is the tale:

"Once, a long time ago, this woman, Kit-si-nao, lived

SKOOLT-KA HAD ONLY ONE CHILD.

there on that island and was happy, for she had many sons and daughters to make her heart glad, and she loved them dearly.

"This was good, for it is well to have many sons and daughters.

"Kit-si-nao was of the Crow totem, and in the same island was another mother who was of the totem of Hootza, the wolf, and who was Skoolt-ka.

"Now this woman, Skoolt-ka, the wolf, had only one little child, and this one was small, and not strong,

THE TRIBE OF HOOT-ZA MET IN COUNCIL.

like the children of Kit-si-nao, the crow, but Skoolt-ka loved it all the more because it was all she had, and was small and weak.

"One day in the moon when birds nest, this child was playing by the lodge door when Kit-si-nao came

THE TRIBE OF HOOT-ZA RAN TO HER LODGE.   119

by and she laughed at it, and made fun because it was
a weak child, and did not run like her children did.

"Then the child began to cry, and Skoolt-ka came
and heard the words of Kit-si-nao. Then her heart
was heavy because of this, and she sat and mourned
a long time, so long that her Tah-mah-na-wis, Hoot-za,
the wolf, came and said, 'Why do you weep?'

"'I weep because my thoughts are heavy with the
words of Kit-si-nao,' said Skoolt-ka.

"'And what are the words of Kit-si-nao, give me the
talk,' said Hoot-za, the wolf, and then Skoolt-ka gave
him the talk of Kit-si-nao this way:

"'Ho! Ho! You are the little one! You do not run.
Your feet are tender, and the stones hurt you. You
must ride on the back of your mother. You have no
brothers and no sisters and you are always by your
mother's door. Why do you not play with the other
children? Because you are afraid. Ho! Ho! You are
the little one.'

"When Hoot-za, the wolf, heard of this talk, he was
angry, and called all of the tribe of the wolves and they
came and sat in a council, and Hoot-za, the chief, told
them of the words of Kit-si-nao and asked what should
be done.

"The tribe of Hoot-za then thought deeply, as the

council pipe was smoked, and then it was decided that Kit-si-nao must be punished for her bad deed of laughing at a little weak child, so the wolves ran to her lodge and killed and ate all the children of Kit-si-nao, the crow mother, because of her bad deeds.

THE STONE WOMAN.

"Then Kit-si-nao was very sad and went up on the mountain where you saw her and wept all the rest of her days for her children who were gone.

"As she sat there, Colesick, the keeper of the dead, came and changed her into stone, and left her there,

as a warning to all people not to laugh at those who
are small and weak, and that is why you saw Kit-si-
nao, the stone mother, sitting there weeping on the
mountain-side by the big water.

"Now, T'solo, the wanderer, the moon makes a short
shadow, and soon Spe-ow will open the daylight box
and your paddle is tired from laying in the canoe.
Come again when Polikely, the night, is young, and
we will have other tales that it is well to know."

So then I left the Talking Pine, and went to my
lodge to wait until another time, and to think about
Kit-si-nao, the stone mother, and her deeds.

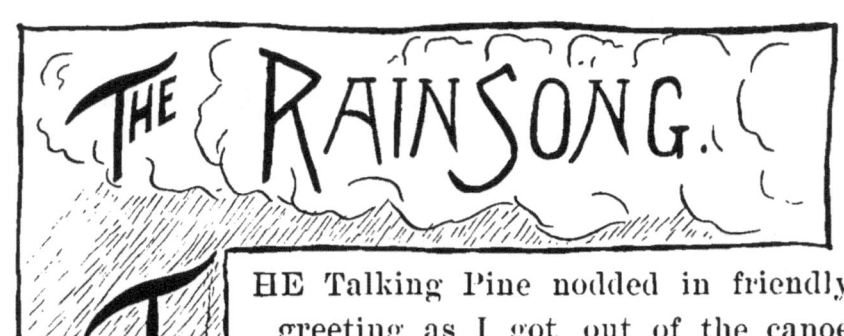

THE RAINSONG.

THE Talking Pine nodded in friendly
greeting as I got out of the canoe
and came up to my usual place at the
foot of the great tree:

"Klahowya, T'solo, the wanderer,
it is well that you came to-day, for to-day the pines
will sing the rain song, and you shall sing with us,
for it is a good song and one to know."

"So be it, Wise One, I will learn the rain song, that
I may know it when I am in other lands. It is a good
song to know when the air is dry, and you can get no
water for your throat. I will learn the rain song of
you, Wise One."

"Come, T'solo, the wanderer, and sit at my feet,
where I can spread my arms over you and keep the
rain away.

"Now when the wind comes all the pines will sing

124

the wind song and dance the wind dance before they sing the rain song. You know, my friend T'solo, that the wind must always come to help the pines sing, so be not impatient to hear the rain song until the wind can help us."

So I sat down by the feet of the Talking Pine, and

SAT AND SMOKED MY PIPE.

smoked my pipe and waited for the coming of the wind to see the wind dance, and hear the rain song.

Soon the wind came slowly out of the Southwest and the pines began to sing and the wind sang with them. At first, so softly I could scarce hear it, and I asked the Talking Pine, "Do you sing, Wise One?"

"Yea, listen," answered he.

Then I heard the wind song, for it had gathered strength as all the pines began to sing, and I could hear it very plainly. Then the pines all began to dance and to swing their long arms in time with the song, and to sway and sing until they were all mad with the dance, and I thought they would fall.

Flowers and Grasses.

The song was wild and mournful, as it always is, and they sing it in the language of the pines, so one must know their talk to learn the words they sing.

I heard them calling the rain to come out from behind the clouds and sing with them. Then the rain rode down with the wind, and some rested on the pines, but most of it went on down and sung with the flowers and the grass; for the rain, you know, is restless and cannot stay long in one place.

The pines all love the rain and always sing the rain

THE PINES DANCED THE WIND DANCE.

song when they see it coming in the clouds, so it will stop and sing with them.

For a long time the pines and the rain sung together, then the rain went away, and the wind went with it, and the pines were left all alone.

The wind, you know, is never tired, and travels all the time, so the pines always call the wind to help them dance, and they always go to sleep when the wind goes away, and the sun wraps his warm blanket around them.

"It was a good dance," said the Talking Pine, when they had finished and the wind had gone.

"Come again, T'solo, the wanderer, and I will show you other things, and sing other songs, but now I sleep."

Then I got in my canoe and crossed the Lake of the Mountains, and left the Talking Pine to sleep out his sleep until another time.

OF WAH-WAH-HOO, THE FROG

'SOLO, wanderer, it is a good night for a tale; Snoqualm makes a path on the water, and the Skal-lal-a-toots put his picture in the lake. Wah-wah-hoo, the frog, sings for his wife among the rushes and the night people call from the shadows of the pines with many voices. It is a night for a tale that has no blood in it, for the smell of blood in the mind is not a good smell with the air of a night such as this. It is a smell for daytime and stories of war, not for times of peace and the full leaf of trees.

"There is a story that goes with the night well, and it is a good tale to know, for it tells of the folly of the young and how it is better to listen to the word of those who are old, and who, by their age, have learned much wisdom. Wisdom is a good thing and it is only the old who are wise, for they are full of years.

"To-night, then, we will hear of Wah-wah-hoo, the

little singer who lives among the rushes over there in the lake."

This, then, the great Wise One told me about the frog, and how he came to be a frog, and you will remember that the frog is a little man, and not kill him when you see him, for some day he will be changed back to his proper shape again, and there will be no more frogs. It is this way:

The Great Chief.

"A long, long time ago, so long that the oldest man cannot remember, there was a great chief, who was the ruler of everything.

"This man was the king of all men, and all birds, and all animals and ruled the world and all in it except another chief, whose name was Klack-a-mass, and who was always at war with the great chief.

"After many years these two got tired of so much war and held a great council talk, for they were Indians, and Indians always have a council when there is an important question to decide.

"This council lasted for many days, and before it was done, the two chiefs had agreed not to have any more wars.

"Then they smoked the great peace pipe and blew the smoke to the four winds, so the world would know

SMOKED THE PEACE PIPE.

they were at peace, and there would not be any more fighting.

"Now Klack-a-mass had a daughter whose name was Kla-klack-hah, the woman who talks, and the great chief had a son whose name was Wah-wah-hoo, the singer.

"When the peace pipe had been smoked at the great council, Klack-a-mass thought it would be well for his daughter to become the wife of Wah-wah-hoo, and thus make the two tribes blood relations and stop any fighting for all times.

"The great chief thought that would be well, too, so it was all arranged for the young folks to get married, without saying anything to them about it.

"After the council was over they were told that on a certain

Wah-wah-hoo.

day they must get married, and thus make the tribes blood relations, as the Indians say.

"Kla-klack-hah thought it was all right and was willing to marry Wah-wah-hoo, but Wah-wah-hoo was very sad, and did not sing his songs any more, for he had long loved a girl of his own tribe named Hah-hah, the one with the bright eyes.

"When Wah-wah-hoo told the news to Hah-hah, she too was sad, for she loved Wah-wah-hoo dearly, and they had planned to be married when the salmon berries were ripe again, which is in the middle of the summer.

"They talked and made all kinds of plans to escape the fate that would be theirs if the Tyee insisted on the mariage of Wah-wah-hoo and Kla-klack-hah, but all these plans were thrown away again because they could not be carried out.

"Closer and closer came the time when Wah-wah-hoo must leave Hah-hah, and go with Kla-klack-hah, and soon there was only one day more.

"Then the lovers met in a dell in the forest to say good-bye and part forever.

"Hah-hah came with her finest dress of tanned and beaded doeskin on, and wore all her ornaments of Hiaqua shells, and over her shoulders she threw a beautiful shawl of woven cedar bark.

"Her hair hung in thick glossy braids and her eyes shone bright. Her cheeks were red and soft, like the skin of a peach, and her smile was all sunshine to Wah-wah-hoo.

"For a long time they sat and talked there among the bright flowers that grew in the dell, and then Wah-wah-hoo said, 'Let us go away in the woods, far away to some other land and live, and forget this place we live in, and forget Kla-klackh-ah. We will find another land and live there always and be happy.'

Carried her into the forest.

"Hah-hah thought for a time and then she said, 'Yes,' and Wah-wah-hoo stood up then and took her in his arms and carried her into the forest.

"For many days they traveled, and at last came to a

great river and a sunny country that was close to the mountains. 'Here we will stop and build a lodge,' said Wah-wah-hoo, 'and we will be safe and can live happy always.'

"So Wah-wah-hoo built a lodge of poles and cedar bark and fashioned a canoe out of a cedar log, with fire and the stone hatchet, T'shum-in, and built spears and traps to catch the wild birds and animals for food.

"Hah-hah wove nets out of the roots of the hemlock tree for Wah-wah-hoo to catch fish with, and she made mats of rushes to carpet the lodge, and blankets of the soft cedar bark to sleep on, and they lived in peace and happiness.

"Now the great Tyee and all the rest of the tribe at home did not know that the young people were gone, so when the wedding day for Wah-wah-hoo and Kla-klack-hah came around, all the people came to the place dressed in their brightest robes and ready for a great merry making.

"Kla-klack-hah wore her wedding robes of beaded doeskin, trimmed with bright feathers and had her hair braided in long braids.

"A great feast was made ready and all the people waited the coming of Wah-wah-hoo to claim his bride.

"The time passed, and though the people waited un-

til the sun went down, Wah-wah-hoo never came, for
he was with Hah-hah then, hurrying away through the
great forest.

"When the sun went down Klack-a-mass, who was
Kla-klack-hah's father, grew very angry at the way his
daughter had been treated, and sent for the Hyas Tyee
to find why Wah-wah-hoo did not come.

"The Tyee came, and when Klack-a-mass told him
the trouble, ordered runners to seek for Wah-wah-hoo
and bring him to the
feast at once.

"All night the run-
ners sought and at
sunrise they reported
t h a t Wah-wah-hoo
was gone.

The Eagle circled high.

"Now they looked
for Hah-hah, and she too was gone. Then the
Tyee knew they had fled and would not come unless
they were caught, and he grew very angry at his son,
who dared to disobey the word of the great chief, his
father.

"Then he called a council of all the animals, and
birds, and fishes, and told them of the doings of his son.

"To the Eagle he said, 'Fly high and watch for Wah-wah-hoo, and do not let him pass.'

"To the fishes he said, 'See that they do not go by you on the waters.'

"He told the chief of the wolves to smell them out.

"The sea gull, the snake, the squirrel, and the chief of the mosquitos were all told to see that the lovers did not pass, and all the other wild things were told to watch that the runaways did not hide.

T'set-shin, the Snake.

"Then the council broke up and the animals began to look everywhere, and it seemed that Wah-wah-hoo and Hah-hah must soon be captured and brought back.

"T'set-shin, the snake, wriggled through the grass and among the tangle of the berry patches to find them.

"Tyee Kula-kula, the great bald eagle, circled high in the air, and looked down over the hills.

"The fishes swam the waters and looked for the canoe of Wah-wah-hoo.

"The squirrels watched among the trees as they ran up and down seeking nuts and pine cones.

"T'kope kula-kula, the sea gull, watched on the sea.

"The chief of the wolves smelled the ground and soon found the lovers, but he remembered that Wah-wah-hoo had once saved his life when he had been caught fast in a trap, so he told all the tribe of wolves not to say where the lovers were.

The Squirrel watched.

"The chief of the mosquitos found them too, but Hah-hah had saved his life once and he, too, told all his tribe to disperse and not say where the young folks had gone.

"Now Ki-ki, the blue jay, who is chief of all the Skall-lal-a-toots, the fairies of the

The Tribe of the Mosquitos.

woods, you know, told all his people to hide the runaways, for he was the friend of Wah-wah-hoo, and so the Skall-lal-a-toots worked to hide them, and to send the animals to looking in other places.

"So the animals looked for many days and did not find Wah-wah-hoo and Hah-hah, and they still lived in the lodge by the great river.

"But the time came when Colesnass, the winter wind, came down from his ice lodge far away in the north, and locked the rivers and the lakes with ice.

"Then Wah-wah-hoo could catch no more fish, and the snow was so deep he could not hunt, and soon

THE WOLVES SMELLED THE GROUND.

there was nothing left to eat in the lodge, and hunger came in the door.

"Then Yelth, the raven, who is the keeper of the fire, came to the lodge and stole the fire, because Wah-wah-hoo could not give it enough wood to burn.

"Colesick, who is the chief of the dead, came and took the life of Hah-hah away, and left her dead, and Wah-wah-hoo was sick in his mind for her.

"Wah-wah-hoo took the body of Hah-hah and went to the great rock that hangs over the pool in the river at the foot of the falls and sung his death chant.

"Then he plunged off into the seething, whirling pool, far below, to die there, because Hah-hah was dead.

"But Wah-wah-hoo did not die.

"The chief of the fishes saw him when he jumped and he took Wah-wah-hoo, and swimming under the ice, brought him to the lodge of the Hyas Tyee, his

PLUNGED OFF INTO THE WHIRLPOOL.

father, and there put him on the shore, and called the Great Chief, who came and found his son.

"Now the chief was still very angry at his son, so he said, 'You have dared to disobey the will of your father, who is the Hyas Tyee, chief of all things. You went away into the woods and left your bride before the wedding day. You are not fit for men and I will change your form. Go and be a frog, and sit in the mud, and sing there always, that I may hear your voice and know that you are afraid of men.'

"So it was that Wah-wah-hoo was changed by his father's magic into a frog, and now he sings at night to mourn for his dead wife.

"Hah-hah is dead, and her shadow looks for Wah-wah-hoo, but cannot find him, because he is a frog.

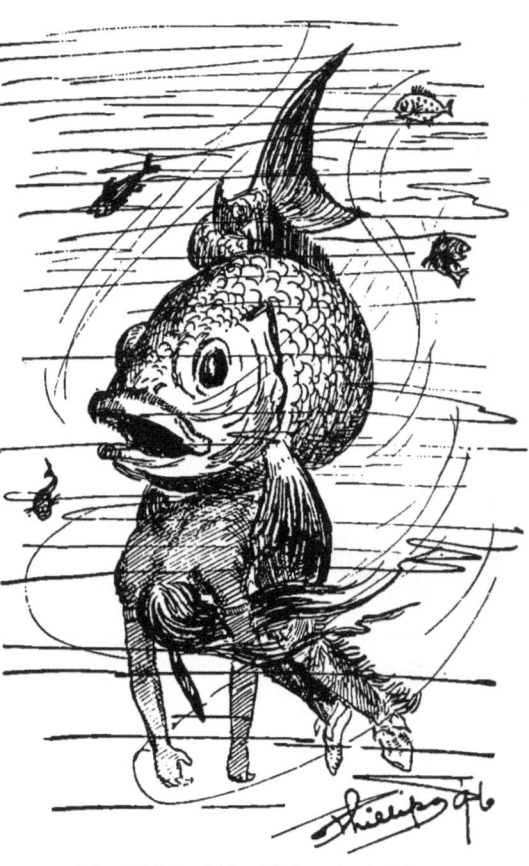

The Chief of the Fishes took him.

"Hah-hah does not know this, and they say she travels over the swamps at night with a strange white light

WHITE MEN CALL HER THE WILL-O'-THE-WISP. 147

in her hand, looking for Wah-wah-hoo, but he is afraid
of the light and jumps into the water, because he is a
frog.

"The white men call Hah-hah the 'Will-o'-th'-Wisp,'
and sometimes they try to talk with her, but then she
only runs away over the swamp and they can never
get near her.

"So now you know who the frog is, and why the Will-
o'-th'-Wisp drifts across the bogs at night, because I
have told you the tale as it was told to me by the Talking Pine a long time ago, away out close to where the
sun goes down by the Lake of the Mountains.

"You will remember now that the frog's real name is
Wah-wah-hoo and that he sings for Hah-hah to come
to him, when you hear his voice at night."

KLOO-KWALLIE MEDICINE DANCE.

HEN the leaves turned brown, the third moon after the ripening of the first salmon berry, I journeyed again to the Lake of the Mountains and smoked the Chinoos until the moon rose; then I went in my canoe across the lake, and when the moon was so high as a pine that has seen but one snow, I sat by the foot of the Talking Pine, to see the sight of the Kloo-kwallie, and watch S'doaks, the son of Yelth, the raven, become a Tah-mah-na-wis-man.

It was a good sight.

A fire was started and soon made to blaze high, that the Ma-sah-chee Tah-mah-na-wis would have his power burned away.

Paints of many colors were brought out and soon all

146

the dancers were painted so bright that the Evil Eye was blind. Spud-tee-dock, the protector, was brought and stood up in the light.

"Listen," said the Talking Pine, and I heard a low

song that came from a long way, and was faint like the voice of the lake when the wind ripples its face, and the Kloo-kwallie was begun.

It was a low-toned song that had not many words, yet those words were not in the Twana language, which was spoken by the tribe of S'doaks, and the Talking Pine told me he did not know the words, though he had heard them many times when he was young.

Louder it sounded and many voices joined in, and then the Klootch-men, who do not dance, wrapped their bark skirts close around them, and sat down to beat drums in time with the chant that

Spud-tee-dock.   the men were singing.

Like the beat of the surf on the ocean sand the song rose and fell, louder, and deep, and full, until a great

noise like the sound of the streets in the town of Squintum, the white man across the mountains, came in the
air and filled it.

That was the song of the Kloo-kwallie, the song that
nobody knows except the wild men who dance until
all are hoo-ie, and their eyes stare and see nothing,
like the crazy folks who have looked on the Evil Eye.

With a great roar of voices and the beating of many
drums came the dancers, all in line, and all dancing
slow.

Each one would jump and then stand stiff like a man
carved from wood, and then jump again. Around the
fire they all moved until they looked like black shadows, and the light from the fire went up in the air and
made bright the arms of the Talking Pine, and no light
showed through the circle because so many were
dancing.

After the men had danced for some time, and the
song was fast and the dancing wild, the Talking Pine
whispered and told me to watch now and listen, for
S'doaks would soon be tested by the fire test.

As I watched the dancers seemed to get pelton,
crazy, the white men say, and two ran up to S'doaks,
and caught him, one by the neck and one by the heels,

THEY LOOKED LIKE BLACK SHADOWS.   149

and they carried him to a small fire that was built to
burn slowly.

Over this fire they held S'doaks, with his back close
to it, until it was cracked and burned, and blisters
came, and caused pain that would make any but a
medicine man moan and cry out.

HELD S'DOAKS WITH HIS BACK CLOSE TO THE FIRE.

But S'doaks had strong medicine and laughed while
his back burned.

Then they carried him back and set him down again
in the circle to dance. As he danced around the medicine fire, and sung the song of the medicine Kloo-

kwallie, the Klootchman gave him sticks pointed with sharp bone, and with these he scourged himself until the blood ran down and dried black against his skin.

"The other dancers lashed his back and arms with switches, and put cedar splinters that blazed like a

WITH THESE HE SCOURGED HIMSELF.

torch against his skin, and S'doaks still danced, for his medicine was strong and his Tah-mah-na-wis made him so he did not feel his hurts.

Until the moon was straight over the head of the Talking Pine, the dance went on, and S'doaks fell down

like a dead man, with his eyes open, but he could not see, for his medicine was gone and he was now like other people and like a man who is mem-a-loose, dead, you know.

Then the Mid-win-nie men, who do not dance, took S'doaks and carried him to the medicine lodge and brought him back to life again, and in time he got well.

The Talking Pine told me that this he must do as many times as he could, and dance the torture dance of the Kloo-kwallie again, before the moon when the birds nest, and that if he did this, and

S'doaks fell down.

his medicine was strong so he would not feel his hurts, then he would be a new Tah-mah-na-wis man, and be one of the Mid-win-nie clan and be a doctor.

This I know he did, for I saw him cure a boy who had looked on the Evil Eye and was already dead, but the medicine of S'doaks was strong and brought the boy back to his body, and made him alive again.

Medicine Pipe.

And this was the dance of the Kloo-kwallie that was danced at the foot of the great Talking Pine.

When it was over I got in my canoe, and crossed back to my lodge, and waited for word to come again from my friend, the Wise One, Ka-ki-i-sil-mah, the Talking Pine.

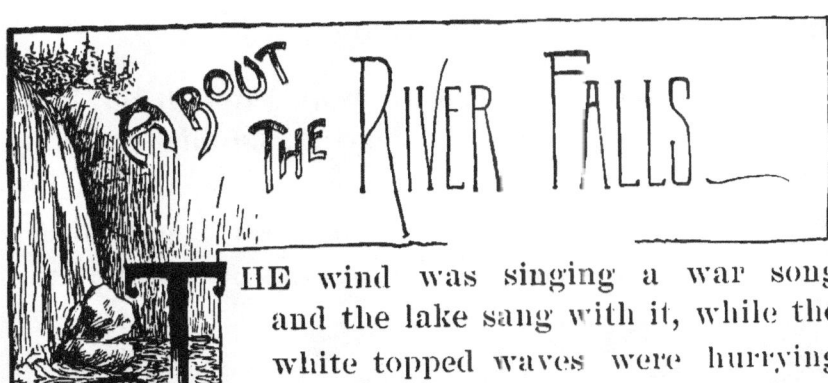

ABOUT THE RIVER FALLS

HE wind was singing a war song and the lake sang with it, while the white topped waves were hurrying against the yellow sand and the restless canoe that bowed and jumped over the water as it looked at the wind.

The voice of the tribe of the pines came to my listening ear in a low murmur from all the mountain side, as they sang the wind song, and the swing of their arms made music for the wind dance.

The great Talking Pine was dancing too, and did not stop his song as I came up from the sandy beach of the Lake of the Mountains, and sat by his feet.

"Rest, T'solo, the wanderer, until the dance is done, and then we will talk," said the Wise One, and so I sat down and looked across the lake at the mountains and at the pines.

The Skall-lal-a-toots are not about when the wind

157

hurries by, and so there were no pictures in the lake, and it was only a sheet of hurrying, singing water.

When the sun sunk into the great water, and the top of Takomah, the great white mountain, began to get like the leaf of a rose, then the wind went away, the

A SHEET OF HURRYING, SINGING WATER.

dancing of the pines was done, and the water began to sleep.

"Now we will hear a tale, T'solo, the wanderer, and it shall be the tale of a river that is by the home of Too-lux, the south wind, and it is a good river, for it

THE RIVER FALLS.

is wide, and deep, and strong. It is the story of the
river falls, Tum-chuck, this way:

"Away back in the time of long ago, this river traveled to the council of the waters just as it does now,
but in one place there was a great bridge of stone that

THE DEMONS FOUGHT A GREAT FIGHT.

was built by the Sah-ha-le Tah-mah-na-wis, so that
men could go over it with dry moccasins.

"This bridge was very strong and very beautiful, and
it was planted with trees and with grass, and there
were flowers and birds there.

"Now in the mountains on each side of the river, there lived two great Too-muck, or demons, and always these demons made magic to kill each other, always, winter or summer, day or night, they made each his cultas medicine.

"After many, many moons, they fought a great battle and the air was black with their breath.

"The ground shook with their fight, and their roars were like the roar of the great water where the waves come against the sand.

"They breathed fire and threw great mountain rocks at one another until the people were frightened and ran away.

"After many suns the fighting stopped and the people came back again, but the beautiful valley of the great river was all changed.

"The grass was dead, the trees were withered, and the great bridge was gone.

"In the place where the bridge had been was only a heap of broken and jagged rocks, and over these the river roared and boiled in anger as it hurried on to the sea.

"No man could pass this place in his canoe, no swimmer could live here for the time of three breaths among the whirlpools, and ever after the great river

NO SWIMMER COULD LIVE HERE.

must fret and groan over the rocks of the broken bridge.

"Far down under the water could be seen the trees that had stood on the bridge, and the Sah-ha-le Tah-mah-na-wis has made them to be stone trees, so that they will always be there, and show where the bridge used to stand a long time ago.

"And this is how Tum-chuck, the falls in the great river, came to be there, and why they will always be there, for the water to sing a war song with as it goes to the sea.

"I am tired with dancing and talking now, T'solo, and would sleep. Come again when the night is young and I will tell you of a great battle of the demons, that was fought by the banks of this same river before Ka-ke-hete was chief of all the demon tribe. It is a good story."

"So be it, Wise One," I answered, "we will have the demon tale sometime, and now I go to my lodge and wish you a good sleep."

Then I went with a lazy paddle across the Lake of the Mountains, and slept until the sun came up over the great mountains from the country of Spe-ow.

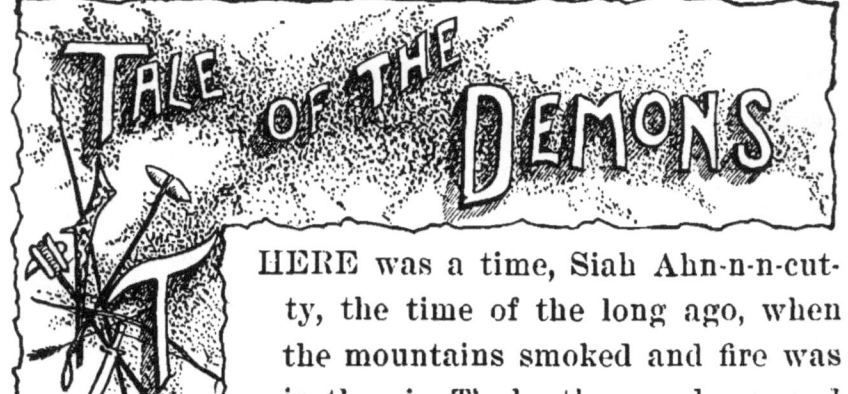

TALE OF THE DEMONS

HERE was a time, Siah Ahn-n-n-cut-ty, the time of the long ago, when the mountains smoked and fire was in the air, T'solo, the wanderer, and of that time there is a tale that we will know this night."

Thus spoke the Talking Pine when I lit the Chinoos in the story pipe and the blue smoke came free.

"My ears listen for the tale, Wise One, and the night comes fast, so speak, and we will know the tale," I answered.

"It is well; this shall be the tale of the demons this way, T'solo:

"In the time when the mountains burned there were no people in the land except the demon people, the tribe of Ka-ke-hete, and they had thoughts only for fighting and for evil ways.

166

"There was a place not far from the place where the river falls were made, the place where I told you of the stone bridge, T'solo, and this place was a great lake like the Lake of the Mountains, but much larger.

"Here was the town of the demons and here they built their lodges along the water.

"Then demons all had long tails, which were very strong, and these they used in battle and they always were fighting.

THE STORY PIPE.

"There was a big demon, who was the worst one, and was the Tyee.

"This one was very strong and had much magic and evil thoughts, but he was wise in many ways, and many times he sat still and thought of other things than fighting while he smoked his Chinoos.

"Now this wise demon saw all his tribe fighting, always among themselves, and he said, 'This is not wise, for sometime they will all kill each other, and there

will be no demons left. It is better to live in peace
and have no more fighting.'

"Once in twelve moons all the tribe came together
and held a big council, and at one of these councils
the demon Tyee made a good talk on the evil of all

A BIG DEMON WHO WAS THE WORST ONE.

this fighting and doing other unwise things that they
did.

"This kind of pow-wow coming from the chief of the
tribe was something that the demons could not understand and they thought he meant evil for them, and

THE BIG DEMON MADE A GOOD TALK.

so would not be a good chief any longer, so all the whole tribe of demons got up to fight the chief to kill him for his ways and this kind of talk.

"Now the chief knew that he could not fight the whole tribe, so he ran away to save himself, and all the demons ran after him.

THE GROUND CRACKED OPEN.

"When he came to the mountains that stood by the side of the lake he struck the ground a mighty blow with his tail, and the ground cracked open, so that the water came rushing in.

"Some of the demons had already got over before the water came in the open place in the ground, and others were caught and drowned, and some could not get across.

"The ones that got across still ran after the chief of all the demons, and so he struck the ground again,

THE GREAT RIVER.

and again it cracked and the water rushed in from the lake. The first few demons got over, but the water caught many more this time and they were swept away.

"Again the chief of the demons struck the ground, and this time it split clear across the big mountains and down to the great waters, and through this crack the water rushed and roared, and made a big river that is the river of the falls as I told you, and is the Oregon, when the white men say the name, and the place of the cracks is called 'The Dalles,' in the talk of Squintum, the white man.

His tail was broken.

"The river carried away the lake and it took the bodies of all the demons clear away to the big water where the sun falls, and now you can see their bones sometimes when the wind makes the great water dig them out of the sand there by the edge of it.

"Now when the demon chief got away and sat down to breathe, he found that the last blow had broken his tail and that it was useless.

"So then he leaped across the place of the cracks,

and went home, for there were no more demons to
fight, and so he did not care about his tail.

"From this family of demons there came all the demons of the tribe of Ka-ke-hete and they were taught
not to fight among their own kind, so they did not
need a tail, and now no demon has one, and they
only work evil deeds on others, and are ruled by Ka-
ke-hete, who is the whistler.

"So this is the story of the demons, and how the
great river came, and it is a good tale, T'solo."

When the tale was finished I took Esick, the paddle, and went to the canoe to go to my lodge.

As the canoe left the sand the Talking Pine called
after me and said, "Come to-morrow, T'solo, and we
will have other tales, and shall know much wisdom.
Klook-wah, til-la-cum."

And so I journeyed away to my lodge by the Lake
of the Mountains, and thought of these things, and
how the river came.

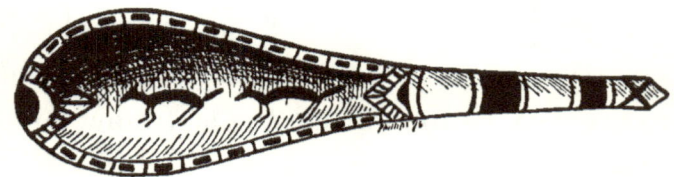

O-NIGHT we will know of the Evil Eye, T'solo, the wanderer," said the great Talking Pine, as I came to my place by his feet.

"It is well, Wise One, tell the tale of the Evil Eye while I listen, Ka-ki-i-sil-mah."

So then the tale was told, and it is like this:

"Know you, T'solo, the wanderer, that the Evil Eye is an evil thing, and that it works evil magic on those who look upon it, and he who has this has also an evil mind and will do you hurt.

"Now if you make enemies with one who has this Evil Eye, then he can work his magic spells and do you great hurt if once you look on his face. This he may not choose to do at the time you look into his eyes, but may do it a long time after, and when he is not near you.

"This power he has so strong, T'solo, that if you are four days journey by canoe away from where he is, he of the evil eye can yet work his magic and do you harm.

"If a man is under the spell of the evil eye, T'solo, then he is pelton, crazy, you know, or his feet do not go as he wants them to, because he cannot make them step like other people can because of the spell. Or he may walk and talk as other men, and then fall down upon the ground and roll there and his eyes stare and see nothing, and foam comes from his mouth, because of the evil magic.

"Now in sickness the Ta-mah-na-wis men know what to do, because they can work spells and find what kind of animal is gnawing at the sick part and then by charms they can drive this animal of sickness away, and make the sick man well, but when a man has looked on the Evil Eye, T'solo, the wanderer, then there is nothing to do for him, because no magic, nor medicine, nor charm is strong enough to break the spell of the Evil Eye.

"The Mid-win-nie men can do good deeds with medicine, T'solo, for they can bring back the life of a dead man from Stickeen, the land of shadows, if they make strong medicine and good charms against Cole-sick, the keeper of the dead, and this I know, for I have seen it done.

THE EVIL EYE.   177

"With the spell of the evil eye it is not so. There is no medicine and no charm that will break this spell, and so the man who has looked on the Evil Eye is no

longer a man, but a man's body, which is mem-loose, dead, and is in the keeping of a Too-muck, a demon of evil who is there by the magic of the Evil Eye, and who is the slave of Ka-ke-hete, chief of all the demons, and must do as he says with the man's body.

"Now when a child is small, T'solo, the charm of the Evil Eye can not hurt it, so there is a way to know

A Medicine Man.

when a man has got an evil eye, and it is this way.

"When a baby comes to the lodge, strap it on a smooth board of cedar wood, and then fasten a hanging strap to the board so the child may be hung up on a peg in the lodge pole and be

A Too-muck.

out of the reach of the Skal-lal-a-toots and always be easy to find.

"Then a rattle must be hung up in front and the

rattlers must be magic rattlers from the medicine lodge.

"Now when a visitor comes in say to him, 'See, I have a strong baby who is always of a smiling face, and laughs at the sound of the rattle.'

Charm Mask.

"The visitor will walk over to see the baby and there hangs the rattle and this he will shake to see if the baby always laughs at it. If the baby laughs then the visitor has good magic, but if the baby cries, it is because of the evil it looks upon in the eye of the stranger, and it is well to get the visitor outside of the lodge curtain.

"That is the way to find the Evil Eye, T'solo, and it can work no spell as long as it is in the same lodge where the baby is, but be very careful that you do not look upon the face of such a man after he leaves the lodge, for then the spell

Medicine Bag.

is on and evil will come unless you always sleep with a Skal-lal-aye mask hung to the lodge pole over your

A BABY OF A SMILING FACE.

head, to work the evil away and keep it outside of the lodge curtain.

"There is a charm to carry in your medicine bag that is a protection against the magic of the Evil Eye too, T'solo, the wanderer, but I do not know what this charm is, and you must give two beaverskins to the Mid-win-nie man to give it to you.

"So remember, T'solo, wanderer, do not look on the face of a man who has the Evil Eye if you would walk straight and never be a pelton Siawash, a crazy man."

This the Talking Pine said of the Evil Eye, as I sat there, and when he was finished I got in the canim and journeyed back to my lodge by the Lake of the Mountains, to think heavy thoughts about the evil ways of these things.

CONCERNING A HUNTER AND A BEAR.

"ONCE there was a great hunter who was Touats," said the Talking Pine, when I asked him for a story.

"Now this man Touats was a great rogue, as well as a great hunter, and he did some deeds that a good hunter should not do, because a good hunter loves the wild things, and is of a broad mind, and a keen eye, and is a good man to the world. But this man Touats was not a good man, for he did not do good deeds.

"This is why:

"Once he traveled a long distance to see the great chief of all the tribe of Hoots, the bear, and came to his lodge.

"Hoots, the bear, was not at home, but his wife told Touats, the hunter, to come in and wait, and soon the bear would come back. So Touats went in and began

184

FOUND HER WITH TOUATS AT THE SPRING.　　185

to talk to the wife of Hoots, the bear, and made love
to her, but she did not like Touats, the hunter, and

The Grouse.

when Hoots came back she
told him of the way Touats
had talked to her.

"This made Hoots very an-
gry and he drove the hunter
away. The hunter did not go
very far, but waited in the
woods until he saw the bear
go on a journey and then he came back to the lodge of
Hoots and again made love to his wife.

"This time she was not angry with the hunter, but
listened to his songs for a long time,
and then Touats went away before the
bear came back.

"When Hoots came back he found
his wife very much confused and afraid
of him, so he suspected that Touats,
the hunter, had been back, and told his
wife that she no longer loved him, but
that she had heard the songs of Touats.

Touats.

"This she denied, though she knew it was so. Hoots,
the bear, still was not satisfied that she had told him
the truth, and watched her go for wood and water for

the lodge, and found that she was gone a long time,
so he tied a magic cord to her robe, and when she did
not come back, he followed this cord and found her
with Touats, the hunter, at a spring.

"Now Hoots was very angry, and to punish his wife

INDIAN DRAWING ON ROBE OF THE HUNTER AND THE BEAR.

for her bad ways he told her he would change her into
a grouse, and so he did, and now she sits in the forest
and mourns all the time because of her bad deeds.

"Then he said to Touats, the hunter, 'You have stol-
en my wife and made my lodge fire cold. You are like

TOUATS AND HOOTS FOUGHT A GREAT FIGHT.   189

Phillips '96

HOOTS, THE BEAR—HAIDA INDIAN DRAWING.   191
Figures on the paws are supposed to represent the Hunter and Bear Story.

T'set-shin, the snake, who crawls in through the back of the lodge and bites when your back is turned. You are not fit to live where there are men, and I am going to kill you.'

"So then Hoots, the bear, and Touats, the hunter, fought a great fight for many days and at the end Touats was dead and Hoots was all alone."

And this was the story of the hunter and the bear that was told by the Talking Pine, and many times since that, I, T'solo, the wanderer, have seen the picture writing of it on many robes and have read it in the carving on the totem poles of the family of the bear.

This story is a good story to remember, for it shows well that those who do bad deeds are sure to be punished and be very sad when it is too late.

DOAK-A-BATL, THE MAKER

ELL me, Wise One, how did the blue jay, Ki-ki, come on the earth?" This I asked the great Wise Pine when I had put the coal of fire on the Chinoos in the pipe, and the smoke was coming blue.

"The tale of Ki-ki, the blue jay, is not a tale of itself, but is the tale of Doak-a-batl, the maker, and to know of Ki-ki, I must tell you the other tale too," answered the Pine.

"Then tell the tale, Wise One, for my ears are open for the tale and I would know of these things."

"Then if you listen, Wanderer, it is the tale of Doak-a-batl, this way:

"Many, many winters ago, there were not many men in the world, and these men were not like the men we

194

see now, for their thoughts were the thoughts of children and they had not many wants.

"After a time the great Tah-mah-na-wis, who was Doak-a-batl, the maker, came up out of the great water where the Sun has his lodge, and walked on the land.

"At this time all the people were living in huts and

in holes in the ground, and in hollow trees, and among rocks near a great river of crystal water which was named Sko-ko-mish.

"Doak-a-batl, the maker, came by this river and saw the people living this way, and he said, 'Why do you live in holes? You should live in lodges.'

"So then he built a lodge of poles and cedar bark and showed the people how to do this to make a house to live in, and they have built them that way ever since.

Doak-a-batl.

"Then Doak-a-batl walked along through the woods until he came to a place where some Klootchmen were catching salmon with their hands, and he said, 'That is not a good way to get fish. Here, I will show you how.'

So he cut many willow poles and with them he wove
a willow weir out in the river in a fashion that would
let the fish in, but would not let them out again, and
in this way everyone could get many fish, and there
would be no one hungry again, and so the Indian
women remembered what Doak-a-batl had showed
them, and they still know how to build the willow trap
for salmon.

"When this was done Doak-a-batl went on and soon

saw some
men on a ce-
dar log,
floating
along in the
water, so he
made them

T'shumin, the Canoe Chopper.

come to the land. Then he made a fire in the
log, and burned it out inside, and he made T'shumin, the canoe-chopper, and showed them how to cut
away the wood, and there was a canoe made for them
to travel in. That is how the red men found out how
to make canoes. Then Esick, the paddle, was made
and all was ready.

"Then Doak-a-batl, the maker, went on and came to
the place which is now a marsh, and which is where

HE WOVE A WILLOW WEIR.

the river ends and the great water is, and there he
slipped and fell.

"Then he cursed the land and made the water come
up and cover it, and there was a great marsh for a play-
ground for Ena-poo, the muskrat, who sits in the sun

A MEDICINE MAN DANCING.

like a little brown ball, and who builds a lodge of
rushes and mud.

"When the marsh came then Doak-a-batl put the
rushes and the cat-tails in it, and showed the women
how to make mats for the lodge floor out of them, and

so it was a good deed, for it punished the land and
made good mats for men.

"After this was done Doak-a-batl went on and soon
heard a great noise, and went to see what it was. There
he found a medicine man who was dancing a foolish
dance, and was singing 'ki! ki! ki!'

"This medicine man had much blue paint on and his
hair was tied up so it stuck straight up on his head,
and he was not a good sight to look at, so Doak-a-batl
said to him, 'What are you doing?'

Enapoo, the Muskrat.

"The medicine
man said, 'I am
making medi-
cine.'

"Then Doak-
a-batl said, 'You
are foolish, and
do not know the ways of medicine, you are not wise
in the ways of Tah-mah-na-wis, and are not fit to be
of the Mid-win-nie clan. For this I will change your
form. Go and be a blue bird, Klale-kula-kula, and be
known to men by your song, Ki! Ki!'

"So by the magic of Doak-a-batl the foolish Tah-
mah-na-wis man was changed and there was Ki-ki, the
blue jay, and he was the first one of that kind of bird.

LEFT THREE BIG TRACKS.   201

"That is why the blue jay has a crest, because the hair is his top-knot.

"Then Doak-a-batl journeyed on to the north and close by the mountains that are by the great water, he stepped on a big flat rock, and left his tracks, three times, and there you will see it now, so that if men forget his deeds, they will always remember them again when they see the tracks of Doak-a-batl in the rock.

"From this place nobody knows where he went, and so Doak-a-batl is gone from the minds of men, and they do not know how he looks, and remember only his deeds."

This was the story of Doak-a-batl as I listened to the tale from the Talking Pine, there by the Lake of the Mountains, in the land of T'set-se-la-litz, the country of the Sundown, a long time ago.

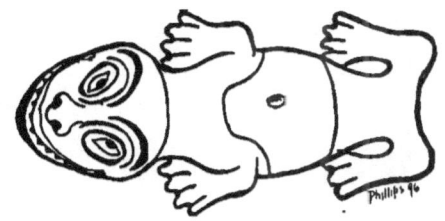

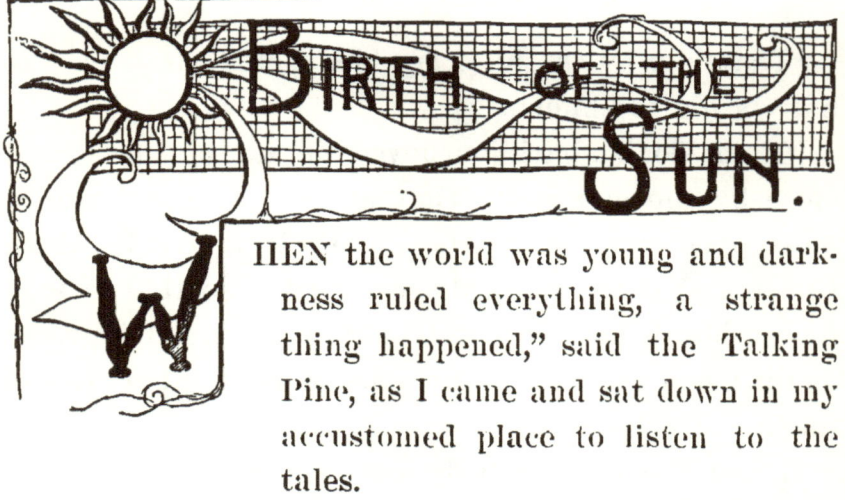

BIRTH OF THE SUN.

HEN the world was young and darkness ruled everything, a strange thing happened," said the Talking Pine, as I came and sat down in my accustomed place to listen to the tales.

"And what was this strange thing, Wise One?" I asked.

"It was this," said the Talking Pine, "this, the birth of the Sun."

"I would hear the tale, Wise One," I answered, and then he told me of this happening:

"A long, long time ago, the world was in darkness and people did not have the sun and moon in the sky to give them light. At this time there was an aged

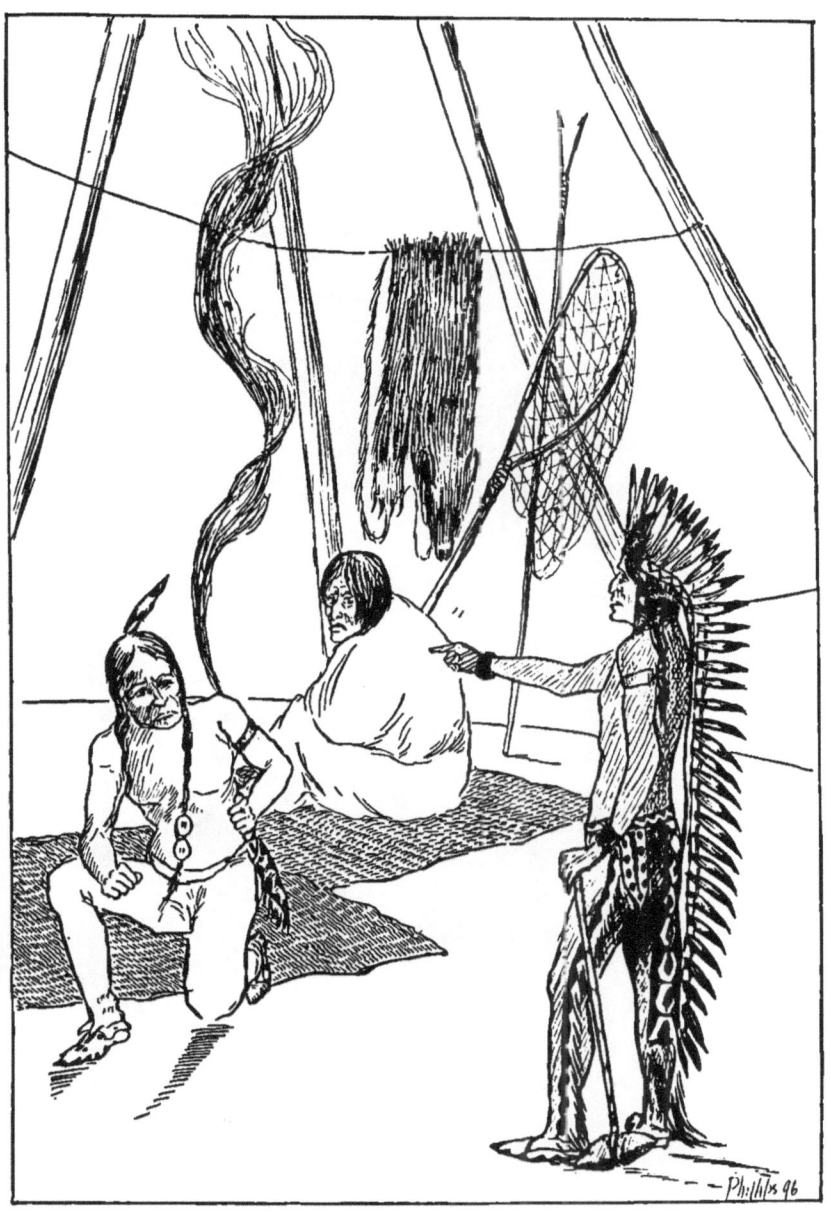

FOUND HIS BROTHER OCCUPYING HIS PLACE.   205

woman who had a son, who was a bright, cheerful boy, and was much loved by his mother.

"This boy went to see his grandmother at one time and stayed with her many days. When he started home again through the forest he was stolen by Ka-ke-hete, the chief of the demons, and carried away beyond the mountains, where, if any one tried to follow, the mountains would close together and crush whatever was between them.

"While he was in the country of the demons the boy learned much magic and became a great Tah-mah-na-wis man, and then by his magic powers, found a way out of the country and back to his own tribe again.

"Now when this boy was stolen, his mother was very sad and mourned for many days, because she thought she would never see her son again, and to comfort her in her loneliness, Spudt-te-dock, the protector, gave her another son.

"The second son also grew to be a bright boy, and was loved by all who knew him, and loved most by his mother.

"Now time went on, and after many snows had passed, the first son came back and found his brother occupying his place at home. Instead of welcoming his brother, the wanderer became angry at him, and said he would change him into the moon, and he should be chief of the night, while he would use his magic and change himself into the sun and rule the day. This he did, and the first day began.

"As the older brother, who was the sun, climbed up the sky, it began to get very hot, for he was very angry and shone fierce and bright.

"Soon the rivers dried up, the grass and trees wilted, and the people began to die of the heat.

"When the sun saw these things, he saw that he was too strong, so he changed things about and made his younger and weaker brother be the sun, and he took his brother's place as the moon, and things went along all right as they do to this day.

The Moon Boy.

"Now you can see the man in the moon on any bright night, and if you could see hard enough, you could see the boy in the sun, but the sun is too bright to look at and the boy is not easy to find. This, then, is how the days and nights started."

THE SUN BROTHER. 209

So said the Talking Pine, there by the Lake of the Mountains, a long time ago, and he is wise and knows how all these things come about.

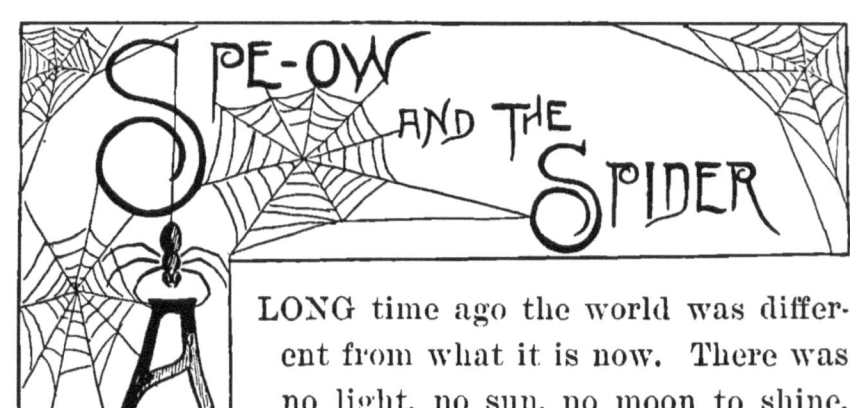

LONG time ago the world was different from what it is now. There was
no light, no sun, no moon to shine,
and no stars to twinkle at night, no
big pine trees, and nothing was as it is now. The people went about in darkness, and did not know what
light was.

"Would you like to know how it was all changed
about so that we now have a beautiful world to live in,
instead of a barren one that is all dark?"

So said the Talking Pine when I got out of my canoe
and sat at the foot of the great tree by the Lake of the
Mountains.

"Yes, Wise One," I answered, "tell me how these
things were changed, and how it all happened, for I

212

would know more of the world and its people who lived before I was born."

"It is well," said the Great Tree, "now sit by my feet and listen, and I will tell you the tale this way:

"When the world was all in darkness, it was ruled over by a strange chief, whose name was Spe-ow, the grandson of Ki-ki, the blue jay.

"They say that Spe-ow was once an Arctic fox, and that Ki-ki, his grandmother, was not satisfied with him that way, and so changed him into Spe-ow, who was a man.

"Now Spe-ow was a very strange man to look at, because he was different from all other men. He was a short, fleshy man, with ears like a fox. His eyes were jet black, but were not like our eyes, for they were placed at the end of horny knobs that stuck out from Spe-ow's brow. A lobster has eyes like the eyes of Spe-ow.

"In his mouth were two great tusks like the fangs of a cougar.

"His nose was sharp and pointed, and he wore a long white beard that reached below his waist.

"For covering he wore a coat made of the skins of the Mountain Goat, and the four buttons on this coat were made of four live blue jays.

"I said Spe-ow was a small man, but really he was a very big giant, only he was a great deal smaller than the other giants who lived at the same time that Spe-ow did.

"Spe-ow could change himself into any shape he wanted to, and could change the shape of other things as well. He could cut himself to pieces and put him-

self together again, and do many other wonderful things. His body could be killed and skinned, but that would not kill Spe-ow, because of his magic.

"This, then, is the strange man who was the chief of the people when the world was all in darkness.

"Now it happened that Spe-ow was walking along one day and came to a place where a beam of light came down from above, and

Spe-ow.

there he saw a rope which hung down from some-where. Then the blue jay came along and said, 'Let us see what this is.'

"So Ki-ki, the blue jay, flew up a little way and called to Spe-ow to climb up on the rope. Up climbed Spe-ow, and up flew the jay, until at last they came

THE MOON CHIEF FOUND HIM IN THE TRAP.   215

to a hole in the sky, and climbed out into another country, which was much like this world is now.

"Spe-ow did not know what might happen to him, or whom he might meet in such a strange country as this was, and thought he had better look around a bit.

"So he changed himself into a beaver and went into a swamp that was close by, to wait and see what might happen.

"While he was traveling through the swamp in the

shape of a beaver poor Spe-ow got caught in a trap and was held fast until the moon chief, who is S'noqualm, came and found him.

"Now S'noqualm thought he had caught a nice, fat beaver when he found Spe-ow, so he took his club and killed

Ki-ki, the Blue Jay.

Spe-ow's beaver body, and took it to his lodge, where he skinned it, and stretched the hide over a bent willow stick to dry, and hung the body up in his lodge to wait until he should want some beaver soup.

"Though his beaver body was dead, Spe-ow was still alive, and he thought he would wait and see what the moon chief would do next.

"While Spe-ow waited, the chief of the spiders came into the lodge of S'noqualm and by their talk Spe-ow found that it was he who had lowered the rope down from the sky to the earth, where Spe-ow found it.

"By and by S'noqualm and the spider went out of

the lodge and S'noqualm soon came back carrying the Sun, the stars, and the box that held the daylight. These he put on a shelf and again went out. Spe-ow thought that was a good chance to make his world bright, so he made himself come to life again, and changed himself back to his proper shape. Then he took the Sun and put it under his arm. The stars he

Spe-ow threw up the Sun.

put under the other arm, and took the box that was full of daylight in his hands.

"Then he ran for the hole in the sky, calling to his grandmother, Ki-ki, the blue jay, to follow him. On the way he pulled up three great pine trees, which by his magic he made small like little bushes. With all these things he started down the rope with Ki-ki, but he was in such a great hurry that he dropped the stars and they scattered all about and stuck to the sky, and there you will see them to-night.

"Spe-ow reached the ground safely with the other things, and at once opened the daylight box and threw the Sun up, in the air, and there was the first day on earth.

"Then he started the pine trees to growing, and soon they covered the whole land like they do in that country now.

"When S'noqualm found that some one had stolen the Sun, and the stars, he was very angry, and went to the hole in the sky and looked down. There he saw Spe-ow at work planting the trees,

S'noqualm fell to the Ground.

and saw the Sun high up in the air, where Spe-ow had thrown it, so he started to climb down and get them back again.

"He only climbed a little way when the rope broke and S'noqualm fell down to the ground, and Spe-ow, by his magic, changed S'noqualm and the rope into stone, and you can see them there to-day, not far from the mountains, and in the great pile of rocks is a face that is the face of S'noqualm, the moon chief.

"Now the moon chief, being dead, made the sky dark, and there was no moon any more until the great Tah-mah-na-wis saw that it was missing and changed the daughter of a wicked old Skall-lal-a-toot into the moon and put her in the sky country. She is still there to make the night light.

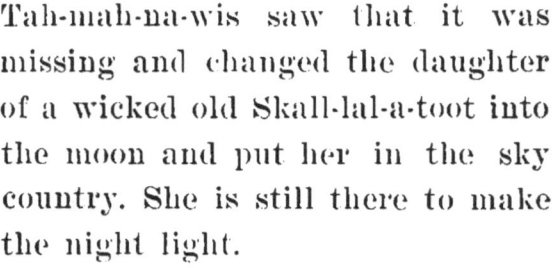

S'noqualm.

"When the spider chief found that his rope was broken and gone, he called his tribe of spiders together, and let them down to look for his lost rope. You can see the spider people even now on warm summer days sailing along on their little ropes that break loose from the sky and let them fall, too.

"They can never find the chief spider's rope, because it was turned to stone by the magic of Spe-ow.

"When Spe-ow got everything to suit him he threw the Sun up into the air every day, and it fell in the great water every night. Then Spe-ow would shut the daylight box and make night, so no one could see him, and go and bring the Sun back.

"When he got back he would open the daylight box to make it morning again, and throw the Sun up in the air.

"This he does to this day.

"Now Spe-ow throws the Sun just the same distance every day, but in the winter, when the rains are heavy and the snow deep in the moun-tains, the rivers are flooded and it takes Spe-ow longer to travel from his lodge to get the Sun, so the nights are long in the winter.

"People don't care for this, be-cause they can't work so well in the winter anyhow, and like to sleep more.

"In the summer time the weath-

The Tyee Spider.

er is warm and Spe-ow don't have so much trouble in traveling, so he gets back to open the daylight box sooner and the days are a good deal longer, so people can do more work then.

"Only once has Spe-ow ever been seen by men, and that was many years ago.

"A party of Indians were camping on Ca-mah-no

island one time, and Spe-ow came upon the bluff above them. He was covered with a curious light like you see in rotten wood sometimes, and when the Indians saw him he was so angry that he kicked half of the island over on the Indian camp and buried it, and so only one man escaped, and he told the story of how Spe-ow looked.

Spe-ow kicked the Bluff over.

"Now all Indians who pass by the place in their canoes mourn and cry for the dead ones, who lie under the water there.

"This, then, is the story of Spe-ow, who lives over across the mountains and is keeper of the Sun."

So said the Wise One, the great Talking Pine, who lives by the Lake of the Mountains, in the land of T'set-se-la-litz, the country of the sundown.

TA-KO-MAH, THE MOUNTAIN

HEN I sat by the feet of the Talking Pine the next time, the sun was just falling down behind the great waters, and there were long shadows on the Lake of the Mountains. The water was red, like the blood that comes from the throat of a killed deer, and there was yellow on the water, too, yellow like Pil-chickamin, the gold that Squintum, the white man, always seeks.

There was blue in the shadow of the pines and blue in the sky where the night was coming; but the mountain, Takomah, the one that feeds, was white and cold over the head of the pines, all white and blue, and very cold, save the top, and this was red, the red of the salmon berry, the red that a great fire paints on the sky at night.

It was a good sight, and I watched it there, so high

223

and grand, and all alone above all the little mountains
that reach only to the snow.

As I sat there my thoughts went far away to other
lands, and other mountains, and my body sat still.
Then the Talking Pine spoke, and then spoke again before I heard him, and this was his speech:

"Know you, T'solo, the wanderer, the tale of the
great white mountain yonder, Takomah, the white one
that feeds, the great chief of the tribe of the mountains?" His voice was far away, like a voice in the
sleep country, where one goes at night, sometimes,
when his body is asleep on the mats in the lodge.

"No, Wise One," I answered, "I do not know the tale
of the great white one yonder, but I see him, once there
with his feet on all the tribe of the mountains and his
head so high that the clouds can only climb half way,
and again I see him in the Lake of the Mountains,
standing on his head like the pines that are painted
there by the water Skall-lal-a-toots. Tell me this tale
of Takomah, Wise One, while I listen and we smell
the smell of Chinoos burning in the pipe."

"Now-itka, oke-oke klosh; yes, that is good," said
the Great Pine, and then he began the tale this way:

"This tale is a tale of warning, T'solo, and it tells
that it is better to take what we have without grum-

THE MOUNTAIN, TAKOMAH.

bling, and so have a good heart, than to want that which we have not, and so not sleep well at night for our thoughts.

"It is the tale of the old man who wished much Ilia-qua, the shell money, and so was taught a great lesson by Tah-mah-na-wis. This is the way:

"Very many summers ago, when my grandfather's grandfather was only so big as a little flower bush, there lived here by the foot of Takomah an old man, a great hunter and fisherman, and one who thought the shell money, Ilia-qua, the best of all things, and this he wanted.

"Always the old man thought how to get more Ilia-qua, and in this he was like the white man, Squintum, who lives across the mountains.

Hia-qua.

"Always this man talked to Tah-mah-na-wis, and always he said the same thing, 'Where can I get Ilia-qua?'

"Tah-mah-na-wis is wise and knows it is not well for men to have a great deal of money; no matter if it is the red man and his Ilia-qua, or if it is Squintum and his gold, it is the same, and it makes men hungry for evil deeds, so the great Sah-ha-le Tah-mah-na-wis did not give to this old man the magic that would bring Ilia-qua, for he knew much Ilia-qua would let Ka-ke-hete, the chief of demons, into the man's mind.

"The old man sat and looked at Takomah as you look at it now, and it was white and cold, and it seemed to know of how this man's great greed for Ilia-qua made him take even the lip and nose jewels of polished Ilia-qua from starving women when meat was scarce, and give them tough and dry scraps of Moos-moos, the elk, in return.

"Now the Tah-mah-na-wis of this old man was Moos-moos, the elk, and one day as he hunted on the side of the white one, Takomah, the old man got very tired and sat down to rest, and as he sat there without any thoughts but rest, he heard the voice of his Tah-mah-na-wis, Moos-moos, the elk, and it whispered magic in his ear.

"This magic told him where to find much Ilia-qua, so much that he could be the richest of all men and be a Hyas-Tyee, a great chief.

"This place was on the top of Takomah, the white one that feeds.

"When this man knew of the place he went back to his lodge and said to his wife, 'I am going on a long hunt.' and then he went away at the coming of night.

"The next night he made his bed just below the snow of the mountain, and when the sun came up it found him on the top.

"He looked down and there he saw a great valley

HE WENT AWAY AT THE COMING OF NIGHT.

in the top of Takomah and all was white with snow but one place in the middle.

"This place was a deep hole in the black rocks and in the bottom of it was a lake of black water.

"At one end of the lake were three large rocks, and

they were Tah-mah-na-wis rocks, for one was shaped like a salmon's head, the next was like a Kamas root, and the last was like the head of his own totem, Moos-moos, the elk.

"Now when he saw this, he knew where the Hia-qua

THE BLACK LAKE AND THE TAH-MAH-NA-WIS ROCKS.

was, so he took his pick of elkhorn and began to dig at the foot of the rock that was like the head of Moos-moos.

"When the pick made a sound against the rock the first time he struck with it, many otters came out of the black lake and sat in a circle, and he counted as many as the fingers of both hands and three more.

"The otters watched him, and at the blow of the pick that counted their number, all the otters struck the ground at the same time with their tails.

"This the man did not pay any attention to, but worked on, and when the sun was just falling into the great water, he turned over a piece of rock and there lay many strings of Hia-qua.

"There were many, many strings, so many that he could not reach the bottom with his arm.

The Elkhorn Pick.

"He would be a rich man and a great Tyee, because no one else had so much Hia-qua as this.

"The otters moved back, knowing he was a child of the Sah-ha-le Tah-mah-na-wis.

"When he had looked long on the Hia-qua and he was sure he had all this for his own, then he put the strings over his shoulder, one after another, until he

could not walk with more, and started to climb back
and go to his lodge.

"Not one string did he hang on the Tah-mah-na-wis
of the Salmon, or of the Kamas, or the Elk, not one,
but started away.

HE STARTED TO CLIMB OUT.

"The otters plunged back into the black lake again
and began to make the water foam and roar, and this
they did until a great storm came and Tootah, the
Thunder, came, and Skamson, the Thunderbird.

"Now everybody knows that Colesnass makes hard

THE WIND THREW HIM OVER THE ROCKS. 233

snows in the mountains, but this time Sah-ha-le Tah-mah-na-wis was angry with the man who loved Hia-qua, and so he helped Colesnass and Tootah to make a very hard storm and he called to the wind to come.

"The wind came and danced around and around, and took the man and threw him over the rocks and the snow, but he still held to his Hia-qua and would not let it go.

"Too-tah, the thunder, roared, and the wind made things black and made much noise, and there was another noise, that was the great anger of the Tah-mah-na-wis, and then came the voice of Ka-ke-hete, the demon, and the small voices of all his tribe.

"All these things said Hia-qua! Hia-qua! and they laughed at the old man and made him afraid, but he still held to his treasure, and tried to go on.

"The air grew darker and very hot, and much smoke came and water ran down the mountain. The wind danced and threw the old man about over the rocks and the snow banks, and the tribe of Ka-ke-hete laughed and yelled Hia-qua! Hia-qua! Hia-qua!

"Then the old man lost his way and did not know which path to take to go to his own lodge.

"Now this man thought to make the anger of the

Sah-ha-le Tah-mah-na-wis to go away, so he dropped one string of his Ilia-qua.

"Just think, T'solo, wanderer, so small was this old man's mind that he only gave one string of all his treasures to the great Sah-ha-le Tah-mah-na-wis!

"The storm grew harder and the air was hot like the breath of the fire, and all the tribe of the demons laughed louder, and great noises came on the wind, and everything said Ilia-qua! Ilia-qua! Ilia-qua!

"String by string the old man threw away his shell money until the last was gone, when he lay down and went to the sleep country.

"It seemed a long sleep, but in time he woke up and found he was on the spot where he had camped the night before he climbed to the top of Takomah.

"He was very hungry and so dug some Kamas roots and ate them, and then he smoked and had many thoughts.

"As he sat there smoking he was huloimie, different, from the man who climbed the great mountain. He was not cut on the rocks where the wind had thrown him, and he was not sore like a man who has fallen down many times, only stiff, and when he moved, his joints made a noise like a lazy paddle on the edge of the canoe.

"His hair was long and white and was like the willow roots that tangle together in the wet sand.

"Tah-mah-na-wis, thought the old man. Now he looked along the side of the great white mountain and it was changed too. New rocks were there that he had

SMOKED AND HAD MANY THOUGHTS.

never seen before, and in places where many trees had been there was only clean, white snow now.

"But most of all, he was much changed in his thoughts and was restful in his mind, for he no longer wanted Hia-qua, and riches had no charm for him.

"Takomah, the great white one, looked down on him and was like a brother, and all the world was glad.

"He had never wakened on a morning that was calmer, and never had Takomah shone so bright and with so many colors.

"He put away his pipe and traveled down the slope of Takomah, but all was new and strange to him, for all was changed.

"When the sun painted the top of Takomah as it paints it now, he came to the foot of the mountain and there was his own lodge, and before the lodge curtain sat an old woman who was singing a low-toned chant, and when he looked close, he saw that this old woman was his wife.

"She told him he had been gone many moons, she did not know how many, and all this time she had traded Kamas root and totem plants and now she had much Hia-qua.

"This old man's mind was not for Hia-qua now, and he was glad to be at his own lodge and at peace.

"He gave whatever he had, Hia-qua and good words alike to all, and the men of all tribes came to him for his counsel, how to spear salmon, how to catch game, or how to counsel best with Tah-mah-na-wis.

"So from this thing the old man became a wise medicine man, and was much loved by all for his wisdom and good deeds, because of his trip to Takomah.

"Then there came a time when he journeyed to Stickeen, the land of the shadows, and his body sat by

AN OLD WOMAN BY THE LODGE DOOR.

the lodge fire alone, and so ended the old man who once loved Hia-qua more than life."

"It is a good tale, Wise One," I answered, "and well to know, for it shows that wisdom is better than all the gold of Squintum, the white man, who lives across the mountains, and who tears up the trees and the grass and builds many great stone lodges all at one place, that he may make Mah-kook, and by this trading get much gold. And now I leave you, Wise One, for the stars say there is not much time left for sleep."

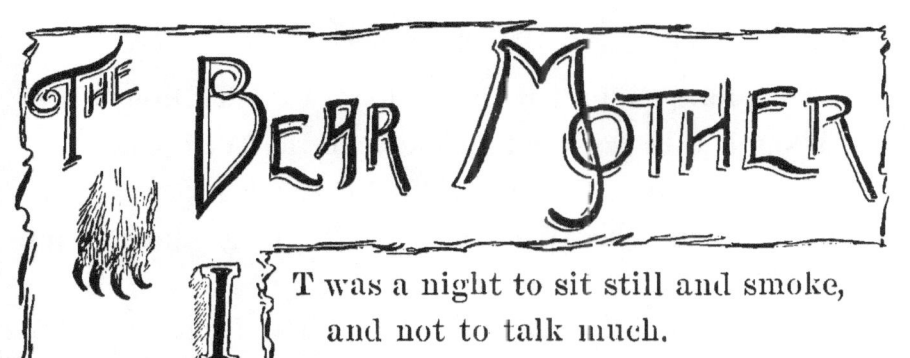

THE BEAR MOTHER

IT was a night to sit still and smoke, and not to talk much.

The Lake of the Mountains was talking a little talk to the sand and whispering to the willows that hung down and dabbled in its waters and over the water the faint song of the Skall-lal-a-toots came, for they were playing among the tall brown water grass that grew at the end of the lake where Ena-poo, the muskrat, builds his lodge.

T'zum chuck kula-kula, the spotted water bird, dived after fishes, and every time he got one he came to the top of the water and laughed like a man who is crazy, pelton, you know. This bird is a Loon, in the talk of Squintum, the white man, who lives across the mountains, and it is a strange bird, for it can sink down in the water and no man can see it come up again; it is of the tribe of Ka-ke-hete, and is a demon.

241

For a long time I sat by the foot of the Talking Pine,
and smoked but did not speak, then the Wise One said,
"What are your thoughts, T'solo, the wanderer, that
you sit down like Wah-wah-hoo, the frog, and say no
word?"

"I have thoughts of the carving that I saw once on
a journey, Wise One, the carving of the Bear Mother."

"Do you know the tale, T'solo?"

"No, Wise One, I have only looked on the carving,

but from this
sight I know
the tale is a
good tale. Do
you know the
story, Ka-ki-i-
sil-mah, wisest
of Pines?"

The Spotted Water Bird.

"Yes, I know the tale."

"Then speak, Wise One, and my ears are open."

"It is the story of the Bear Mother, this way, T'solo:

"There was once a woman who was the daughter of
a great chief, and who was very proud.

"One time in the moon when little birds learn to fly,
this woman went with many other women of the tribe
of T'hlingits, to gather shot-a-lilies, the huckleberries

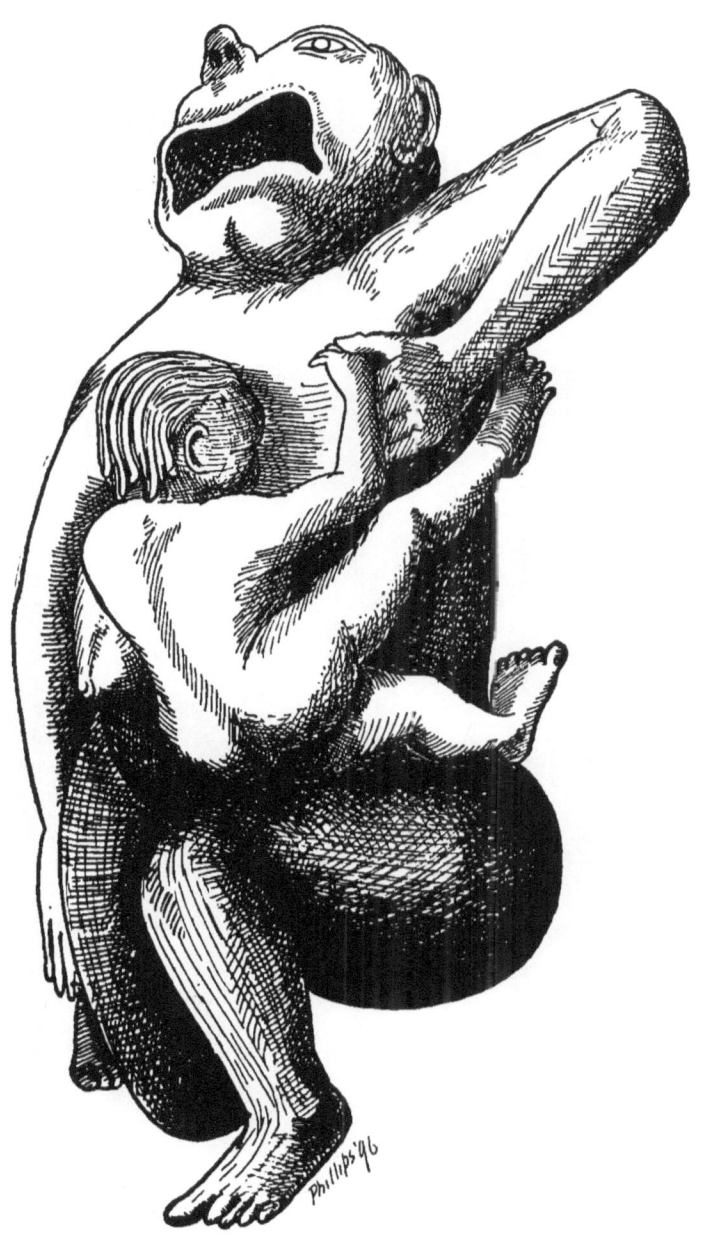

INDIAN CARVING OF THE BEAR MOTHER.   243

that grow in the woods, and which the Indians pat into cakes and dry for the time of Colesnass, the winter.

"Hoots, the brown bear, came to gather berries, too, and the women all made fun of him, because of his

THE WOMEN MADE FUN OF HOOTS.

heavy shape, and his slow ways, and the chief's daughter made more fun than any.

"Now Hoots, the bear, got very angry and killed all of the women except the chief's daughter, and her he carried away to his lodge and made her his wife.

"For a long time Hoots, the bear, kept the chief's daughter in his lodge, and she came to be like the bears, too, then a baby was born, and this baby grew to be the head chief of all the tribe of Hoots, the brown bear.

"Then a party of the tribe of T'hlingits came through the woods hunting for meat, and killed Hoots, the bear, whose eyes were old, and they were going to kill his wife, but she called out to them, and they saw that she was not a bear, but a woman, and they took her back to their lodges.

"In time she told the tale and so everyone came to know it, and it was cut in the totem poles, and carvings were made that are carvings of the Bear Mother and the baby that was half man and half bear.

"When she came back to the tribe of the T'hlingits, the woman married a man of the tribe, and they took the bear for their totem, and so from them came all the people that have the bear for their totem now.

"So this is the story of the Bear Mother that you saw in the carving there on your journey, T'solo, the wanderer.

"Now it is time for men to sleep, T'solo, and you must be in your lodge if you will see the sun come over the mountains in the morning."

HOOTS CARRIED AWAY THE CHIEF'S DAUGHTER. 247

KILLED HOOTS, THE BEAR.

249

So I left the Talking Pine and journeyed to my lodge across the Lake of the Mountains, and on the way I saw T'sing, the beaver, who struck the water twice with his tail to tell his tribe that a canoe was on the water, and then he sunk down to the bottom of the lake and ran to his lodge among the rushes and the white water flowers.

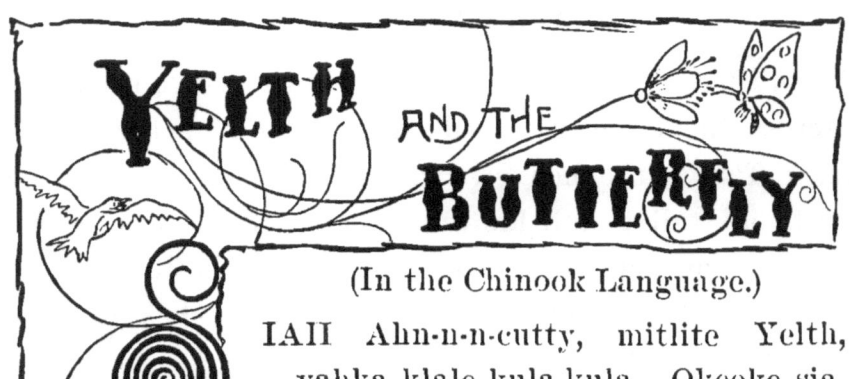

YELTH AND THE BUTTERFLY

(In the Chinook Language.)

IAH Ahn-n-n-cutty, mitlite Yelth, yahka klale kula-kula. Okeoke siawash mamuke konaway ictas siawash ticka, pe konce iskum konaway siawash mamuke, yahka klatawah spose klap cahr konaway siawash mitlite skookum illahee.

Hoots tumtum klosh, pe comtox cahr hiyu skookum muckamuck ictas mitlite.

Copo Yelth klatawah yahka tenas kula-kula, pe konce mesika klatawah siah, yahka tenas kula-kula nanage cahr yahka Hoots mamuke copo illahee pe wawa copo Yelth, 'Cahr mitlite yahka Hoots, yowah skookum illahee pe skookum muckamuck,' pe Yelth closh nanage copo okeoke illahee. Okeoke skookum illahee, pe yowah Yelth lolo ict siawash. Konce chaco

252

HOOTS KNOWS WHERE GOOD EATING IS.   253

copo ict illahee kwonesum kahkwah, yowah lolo ict
siawash, pe wake lalie halo siawash mitlite copo cultas
illahee.

"Okeoke ict ictas Yelth mamuke siah ahn-n-n-cutty,
pe yahka hias skookum Tah-mah-na-wis kula-kula,
nah?"

TRANSLATION OF YELTH AND THE BUTTERFLY.*

Long ago lived Yelth, the black bird.

He made (or got) all things that Indians want, and
when he got all men made, he traveled (supposing)
to find where all Indians could live (in a) good
country.

Hoots (the brown bear) knows (or has) good
thoughts and knows where good eating is.

With Yelth traveled the little butterfly, and when
they (had) traveled far the butterfly saw where Hoots
(the bear), (had) dug in the ground, and he said to

---

*To read the translation verbatim as nearly as it is possible to ex-
press it in English, leave out the words enclosed in parenthesis,

Yelth, "Where lives Hoots, there (is) good land and good eating" and Yelth looked well on this land. That was (a) good land and there Yelth carried one Siawash (tribe). When (they) came to one (more) land like this, there he (Yelth) carried one (more)

THEY SEARCHED FOR HOMES FOR THE TRIBES OF MEN.

Siawash (tribe) and soon no Siawash-(es) lived in bad countries.

This (is) one thing (that) Yelth did (a) long, long time ago, and he (is a) good magic (working) bird.

Don't you think so?

KLALE TAH-MAH-NA-WIS

AS I sat in my lodge by the Lake of the Mountains the wind called to me as it hurried by and said this message from the Talking Pine:

"Come to-night, T'solo, the wanderer, when the face of Sno-qualm shows over the snow of the mountains, for there is to be a Klale Tah-mah-na-wis, and it is to be here by my feet.

"It is a good sight and may not be seen again in the time of men, for Squintum, the white man, says the Klale Tah-mah-na-wis must stop, and Squintum is as the grass blades for numbers, while the red man is weaker each year, like a willow that can get no water."

So said the Talking Pine by message brought by the wind.

I sat and thought on this while the Chinoos burned,

257

and when there was no more, I called to the wind and
gave him this message for my friend, the Wise One:

"Say to Ka-ki-i-sil-mah, the Wise One, who stands
alone; say that T'solo, the
wanderer, will come to-
night when the face of Sno-
qualm makes light on the
snow of the mountains, and
we will see the sight of the
Klale Tah-mah-na-wis.   It

Tah-mah-na-wis Wolf Mask.

is well, and now the grass dies for want of light, because of your shadow on it."

So then the wind went away and I waited for the
face of Sno-qualm to come over the mountains.

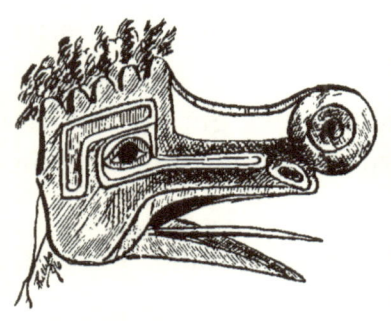

Tah-mah-na-wis Wolf Mask.

When the little night bird*
without feathers began to fly
after bugs and Polikely Kula-
kula began to call for his
wife from the limb of the
dead pine, I got in the canoe
and journeyed to where my
friend stands

"You are in good time," said the Wise One, "for I
hear the sound of many paddles and soon the red men

*The Bat.

THE KLALE TAH-MAH-NA-WIS DANCE.

will build the dancing fire, and we will see the magic
dance, the Klale Tah-mah-na-wis, that is part a secret
that nobody knows but the red men who are of the
black magic totem."

And so I sat and waited until the red men came.

Soon many canoes were drawn up on the sand and
many men came around in the open place by the feet
of my friend, the Wise One.

A fire was made and the smoke went up and hid the
top of the Talking Pine with its blackness and the
night was bright with firelight. Then many men sat
where the light would shine on them and some went
out in the darkness, and from these we soon heard a
chant.

"That is the song of Klale Tah-mah-na-wis, the Black
Magic," said the Wise One, "and soon we will see the
dance, for they are ready to begin."

Then came a strange sight.

One man came running up by the fire, then another,
and still others, until there were as many as all the
fingers of both hands and that many more, and some
of them were very strange, for they were painted with
bright paints and had no blankets on.

Each of these was led by another man who wore

his robes and held a long string of skin and to this a painted man was tied.

The painted men each wore a mask and made strange noises, so I said to the Wise One, "Why is this, and what does it mean, Wise One?"

"It is Klale Tah-mah-na-wis, the Black Magic, and each man who is painted is to be a bird or an animal in the dance, and all will be made members of the clan of Black Magic before the dance is done, and that part we cannot see, for it is secret and no man may look upon it if he is not of the Black Magic clan too, so when this time comes you must get in your canoe and go to your lodge or the red men may kill you, for they are pelton with the dance, and do not know what they do."

Tah-mah-na-wis Mask.

So said the Talking Pine.

Now I looked close and listened, and so I heard the voice of Ki-ki, the blue jay, and the voice of Tyee Kula-

Thunderbird—Tah-mah-na-wis Mask.

kula, the great gray eagle, and many other voices, and these voices came in the chant of the painted men.

I saw one who jumped like Wah-wah-hoo, the frog,

A SKALL-LAL-A-TOOT. WOODEN FIGURE USED IN THE KLALE TAH-
MAH-NA-WIS DANCE. 263

one who ran like T'sing, the beaver; another was like Itswoot, the black bear, and one like Hoots, the brown bear, and Hootza, the wolf, was another.

These I could see by their acts, and by the mask they wore over their heads, and there were many more, like Skamson, the thunderbird, and Yelth, the raven, and all were dancing.

Tah-mah-na-wis Wolf Mask.

As I sat and looked at the dance I saw Hootza, the wolf, run at a man and snap with his mask, like the real wolf does, and Hoots, the one who was the brown bear, danced on his feet and swung his arms as the bear does when he stands on two legs.

The one who was T'sing, the beaver, ran on his hands and feet and gnawed at sticks with his mask,

Tah-mah-na-wis Mask.

so all could know he was T'sing, the beaver, and the one who was Skamson, the thunderbird, made his arms go in the air like the wings of Skamson and beat on a drum to make the song of Tootah, the thunder, and all knew who he was.

All these men danced around the fire for a long time, the ones who wore no masks holding the strings fastened to the painted ones, who were the animals, and

THE DANCERS SAT DOWN.

they did many things that made all who saw them laugh, because they did like birds and animals do, and there was no evil.

When the moon, Sno-qualm, made all the shadows short, and the dancing fire had burned low and was red, then the dance stopped, and all the rest of the red men except the dancers got in their canoes and began to paddle away.

The dancers sat down and began to chant a low-toned song, and then the Talking Pine spoke, "It is time to go away, T'solo, for now the red men do secret things that no man may see and live, if he is not of the Black Magic clan. I cannot tell you of these things and you would not be wise to stay here,

The Thunderbird—Tah-mah-na-wis Mask.

so go in your canoe and do not come back until to-morrow night, for these men will soon be like men who have looked on the evil eye, and it is not good to see."

So then I got in my canoe and journeyed to my lodge across the Lake of the Mountains, and left the red men there singing the chant. That night I did not go to the sleep country, but lay on the lodge mats until Spe-ow threw the Sun up and opened the daylight box, and all night the sound of the chant came across the lake on the wind, sometimes low and far off, and sometimes wild and fierce, and all night the top of the Wise One was red with the fire-light that burned for the Klale Tah-mah-na-wis.

What deeds were done there I do not know.

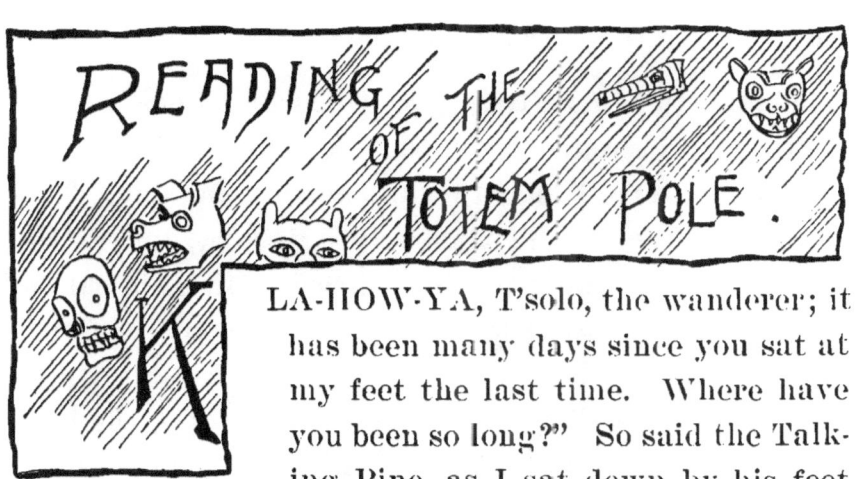

READING OF THE TOTEM POLE.

"LA-HOW-YA, T'solo, the wanderer; it has been many days since you sat at my feet the last time. Where have you been so long?" So said the Talking Pine, as I sat down by his feet and rested from my journey.

"I have been on a journey to a strange land, and I have looked on strange men, Wise One, and I am weary. My paddle, Esick, is tired of traveling, and my canoe is heavy from being so long in the water.

"I have seen many strange things, and have looked on strange totem poles, which I do not know the reading of. One of these I have here in the canoe, Wise One, and I will set it in your sight that you may read the tales that are cut upon it."

Then I went to the canoe and carried the great totem pole up where the Wise One could look on the carvings and read the stories for me as I smoked. When the Wise Pine saw the carvings he said, "This came from some one who was a Iliada, and of the tribe of Hoots, the great brown bear, for he is carved at the top and is the totem of the owner of the house that this pole stood by.

"This you may know because of the ears of the bear which are carved to look like the ears of Hoots, though the body is more of a man's body, and has hands and feet like a man. This is so because the Indians say that the great chief of the bears is a man who has the head of a bear, and so they carve him that way for the totem of the bear.

"Now you see, the figure of Hoots, the bear, sits on three rings carved on the pole. This means that the man who owned this pole was rich and had given three feasts and dances to all the rest who were of his tribe, and so you see it cut there that no man may forget it.

"Below the rings I see the great Gray Eagle, and this carving means Tah-mah-na-wis and is good medicine for the owner and all his household and no man knows what it is but the owner.

"Then I see Yelth, the raven, and in his mouth he

THE GREAT TOTEM POLE.   271

holds the moon which he stole from the eagle, his uncle, and he holds the dish of fresh water between his feet. Now this carving is the story I told you once here when the chinoos burned and Sno-qualm, the moon, climbed up the sky, and it is cut there that men may not forget the deeds of Yelth, who got these things for the use of men.

"Under the carving of Yelth is the story of Touats, the hunter, and Iloots, the bear, cut in the pole, and by the feet of Touats are two otter heads to show who he is. This tale I told you, too, a long time ago, and now you see it carved in the totem pole of a man of the bear totem, because all men of this totem know the story and it is cut there that their children may read it and not forget the tale.

"Next is the carving of T'sing, the beaver, and this you may know by his teeth, for they are always cut like the teeth of T'sing. Now this is the totem of the man's wife who lived in the house, and it is cut there that the woman may not forget her own people, who are of the beaver totem, and so her children may know to what tribe their mother belonged.

"So now, Wanderer, you know the reading of the carved pole that you got in your journey, and I know by seeing it that you have been to the North, by the

home of Colesnass, the winter, for this pole was carved
by a man who was of the tribe of the Iliadas, who live
by the great water, far away toward the cold country. Where did you get the pole, Wanderer?"

"I was on my journey in the canoe, Wise One, and as

THE LODGE OF THE DEAD MAN.

I paddled along by an island in the great water that
is far away toward the cold country of the North, I
saw this pole standing among the pines. I went to
the shore, for I had thoughts that there were people
near it and I went there.

I BROUGHT THE GREAT POLE FROM THE CANOE.

275

"There was the pole and a lodge that the wind and the rain had torn and broken, so no one could live there, but there were no people.

"Then I read the signs, and this I found: There had been a family living here by the pole, and they had built this lodge. There was a man and his wife and one small child who had lived in the lodge, but who were dead, memaloose, for I saw their bones there, all white in the sun, because they had journeyed to the land of the Stickeen many moons ago. There was a canoe there, all split by the sun so that small pines grew up through the cracks, and on the head of the canoe was cut the totem of Hoots, the bear, so I knew that it was a man of the bear clan who had built the lodge.

"I knew that the man was rich, because many blankets and many robes were piled up in the lodge, but they were rotten from the wet. As I read the signs and walked around I found this medicine rattle hung up in the lodge, and it is carved with things that I do not know, so I will leave it in your sight that you may know what is cut on it and tell me when I come again.

"Then I went to this totem pole, and put my hand against it and it fell down, for it was so old that the wet had rotted it at the ground and made it ready to break.

"When it fell I carried it to the canoe and brought it here that we might read the story of the man whose

bones w e r e there in the sun, and who had been dead f o r m a n y moons, for his bones w e r e white l i k e the arms of a dead pine."

"You a r e good in read-ing s i g n s, T'solo, a n d have told the story of the dead m a n.

THIS IS THE TALE.

Your eyes are keen and you see small things. Go now to your lodge and come again on another night, and then I will read the carvings on the medicine rattle, for they tell strange things."

So then I put the great totem pole back in the canoe and went across the Lake of the Mountains to my lodge, and there I set the carved pole in the ground, as it stood by the lodge of the dead man in the country of the Hiadas, far to the North.

CARVING OF THE MEDICINE RATTLE

WHEN I went again to the Talking Pine he told me the story of the carving on the medicine rattle that I brought from the lodge of the dead man in the Iliada country, where I got the great totem pole that stands by my lodge.

This the Wise One said of the rattle:

"This rattle is of the Mid-win-nie clan, T'solo, and so I know that the dead man whose bones you saw was of the medicine clan, for no other can use a rattle like this, and it is for driving away Skall-lal-a-toots from the medicine lodge, and has many totems cut on it.

"This one at the end is the head of Yelth, the raven, and you see the stick in his mouth that he used to carry the fire on to the lodges of men, as I told you a long time ago. The head of Yelth is cut on the rattle,

280

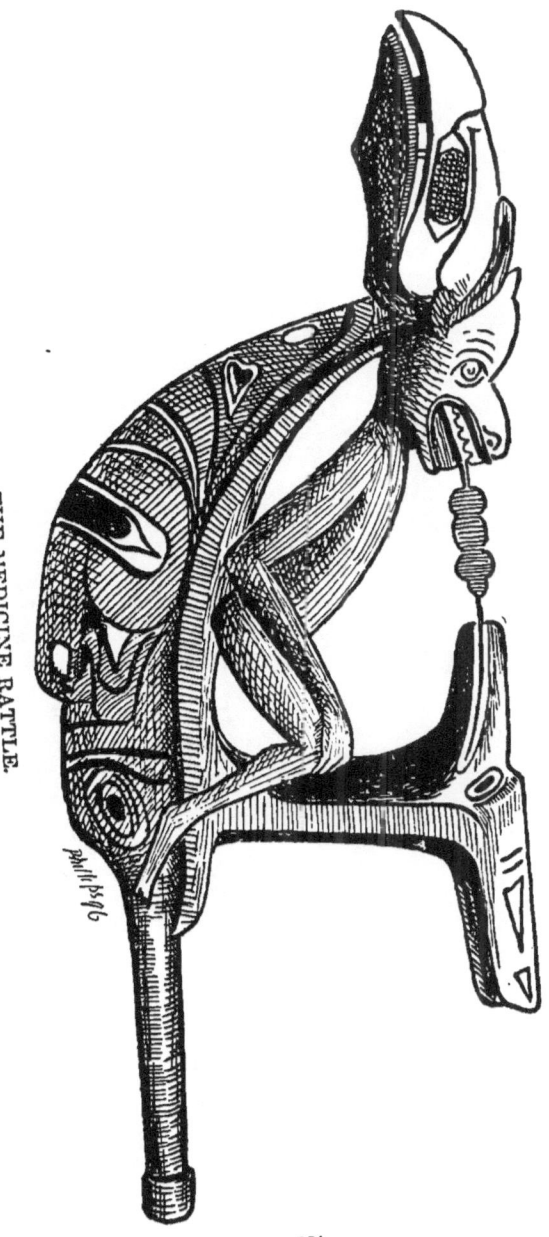

THE MEDICINE RATTLE.

281

because it is a sign of good, and is a good totem.

"The breast of Yelth is made like the breast of the sparrow hawk, and the head of the sparrow hawk is where the tail of Yelth should be, and in the hawk's mouth is a carving of Wah-wah-hoo, the frog.

"Now that is because the hawk is a medicine bird, and it carries Wah-wah-hoo, the frog, to the medicine men so they may get medicine for working evil from

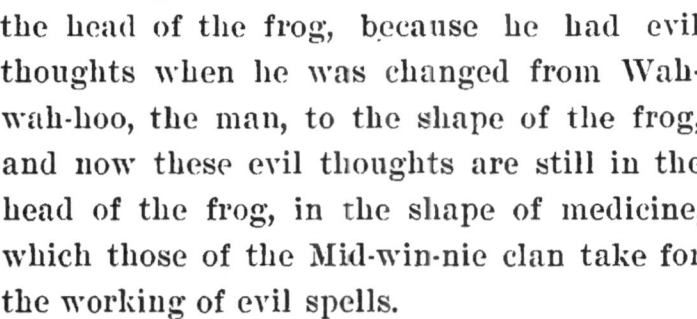

the head of the frog, because he had evil thoughts when he was changed from Wah-wah-hoo, the man, to the shape of the frog, and now these evil thoughts are still in the head of the frog, in the shape of medicine, which those of the Mid-win-nie clan take for the working of evil spells.

Medicine Rattle.

"On the top of the rattle I see Ka-ke-hete, the chief of demons, and a girl who is in the form of Ki-ki, the blue jay.

"Now you see there is a frog again going from the mouth of Ka-ke-hete to the mouth of the girl, and this means that Ka-ke-hete is talking a lie to the girl and it is a lie about the blue jay, Ki-ki, and means evil for the girl to be seen listening to the talk of Ka-ke-hete, for he is the chief of demons.

"The whole rattle is the carving of the raven, Yelth,

who is the totem of all the Iliada tribes, and is for good
medicine, and you must hang it to your lodge pole for
a charm against evil things.

"That is the reading of the medicine rattle, T'solo."

So when the Wise One was finished I took the rattle
and went to my lodge across the Lake of the Mountains, and hung it there for a charm against evil spirits that travel in the night.

SKAM-SON, THE THUNDERER.

HEN the canoe grated on the sand and I came up from the Lake of the Mountains the next time, the great Talking Pine was silent until I spoke.

"Do you sleep, Wise One?" I asked as I took my accustomed seat ready to listen to the tales.

"A-he, Snugwillimie T'solo," he answered, "I sleep the sleep of the old, for I am weary of the dancing and of play. To-night the sky is clouded and the water is black with shadows so that you cannot see the mountains that the Skall-lal-a-toots paint, for they paint only when there is red in the sky at evening, and when there is blue in the sky in day.

"To-night is a night of rain, and soon Skamson, the great thunderbird, will flap his wings and then you will hear Tootah, the thunder, sing his war song, and you will see Chethl, the lightning, who is the glance of the thunderbird's eye.

"Tell me of the thunderbird, Skamson, and of his deeds, Wise One, for this I do not know, and have heard only t h e story of how he was born there by the great river.

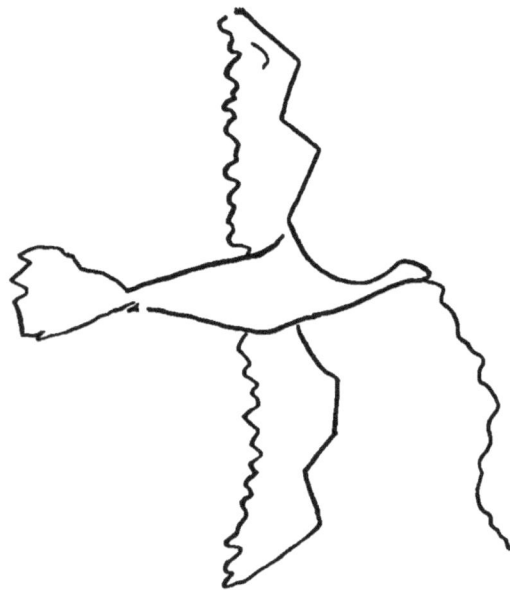

"It is a good night for the tale of Skamson, and I will tell you of him, T'solo, t h e wanderer, if you listen well. It is like this:

"You know the tale of how he came to be, so of

Indian Drawing of Skamson.

that I will not speak, but will only tell of his deeds as they were told to me by S'doaks, the Twana medicine man.

"Now Skamson, the thunderbird, is a man who is in the shape of a bird, and is the keeper of Chethl, the

THE FLIGHT OF SKAMSON.

lightning, and the keeper of the medicine plants, for he makes the rain and so makes all the medicine plants to grow.

"Skamson eats nothing but whales, and these he does not have near his home, which is on top of a high mountain, where he sits wrapped in his robe of clouds.

Indian Drawing of Skamson.

"Because he eats whales he must go to the great water to get them when he is hungry, and that is why we have rain, this way:

"When Skamson feels hunger then he makes magic and many clouds come in the sky, so that Skamson may fly to the great water behind them and not be seen by men.

"By and by the clouds cover all the sky, and when the thunderbird, Skamson, starts on his journey and

flies like a bird, with his eyes looking straight ahead
and his great wings flapping, then you hear the war
song of Tootah, the thunder, for that is the flapping
of the wings of Skamson.

"Sometimes as he travels to the great
water Skamson looks down through the
clouds and Chethl, the lightning, throws
a piece of fire down to the ground to
make a hole in the clouds, so that Skamson may see through, for Chethl is keeper of the eyes of Skamson, the thunderbird, and lives in the head of Skamson.

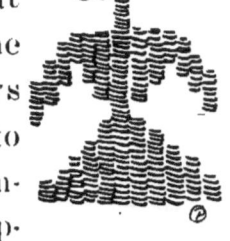

Indian drawing of
Skamson.

"When the thunderbird gets to the great water and
sees a whale, then Chethl throws fire down again and

kills it for food for Skamson, and
sometimes this fire hits a man by
mistake and kills him, as it does
the whale.

Indian drawing of
Skamson.

"After the whale is dead then
Skamson takes it with his feet and flies to a high
mountain to eat it, and then the rain does not fall any
more, and Tootah, the thunder, is still.

"Now there is an island in the great water far to the
North, in the country of the Haidas, and on this island

is a high mountain and there are many bones there, for that is the place where Skamson has eaten many whales.

"Skamson is a very large bird-man, for an Indian of the Twana tribe saw him rest on a high mountain once, and this Indian tied one of the feathers of Skamson's wing to a tree, so that when the great thunderbird flew away the feather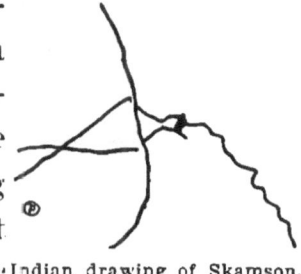

Indian drawing of Skamson.

was pulled out, and when it laid on the ground it was the length of fifty canoes, and so it was very large.

"This feather was made into medicine and is in the medicine bags of the tribe of the Twanas to this day, for it is strong medicine and works good.

"Skamson, the thunderbird, is a great traveler, and so the men who live across the mountains by the land of Squintum, the white man, know of his deeds, too, and have him pictured on the robes in the medicine lodge of many tribes, and these picture robes you may see among many tribes, even so far as five great lakes that stand close together in the country of Squintum, the white man, and where now no Indians live,

War Club.

because of the white man, who lives all over the land there by the lakes.

"But one time long ago many tribes lived by these lakes before Squintum came, and these tribes all knew of Skamson and had his picture painted on the robes.

WHERE THE WHITE MEN LIVE BY THE LAKE.

"Here the Indians cut the carving of Skamson on their war clubs to give them luck in hunting, because he is a Tah-mah-na-wis spirit, and they cut the carving on the canoe stem that it may find good fishing for them, and they paint it on their lodges, and tattoo it on their arms, because of its magic.

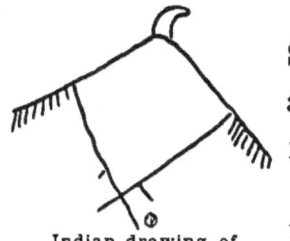

Indian drawing of Skamson.

"And this, then, is the tale of Skamson, the great thunderbird, as it was told to me by S'doaks, the medicine man.

"Now it is time to journey to your lodge, T'solo, the wanderer, for Skamson has started on his way to the great water, and soon the rain will fall, and I hear the war song of Too-tah, the thunder.

"You must have good eyes to see to-night, T'solo, else you will miss your way across the Lake of the Mountains, for darkness hangs thick over the water.

Indian drawing of Skamson.

"Now Klook-wah, tillicum, and come again, for I

Indian drawing of Skamson.

must sing the rain song and dance the wind dance, and have no time for talk."

So then I left the Wise One, and journeyed to my lodge across the Lake of the Mountains, and as the door curtain fell behind me, I heard the war song of Too-tah, the thunder, and then rain began to fall.

THE SING-GAMBLE

AS I sat in the door of my lodge by the Lake of the Mountains, I looked toward the great Talking Pine, and saw the light of a fire flare up, and make his great limbs shine in the dark, so that I wondered what was happening there.

Soon I heard voices, faint and far away, as they came over the lake, and these voices were the voices of men who sang a wild chant which I could not hear the words of. After I sat and listened for some time I got Esick, the paddle, and went down to the canoe, for I wondered what deeds were being done there by the foot of Ka-ki-i-sil-mah, the Wise One.

Slowly I paddled along, and by and bye the canoe went softly against the yellow sand, and I left it there while I went up to see why the fire burned.

"Kla-how-ya, T'solo, the wanderer," said the Wise
One, "you come at a good time, for now you will see
the gamblers, and hear the song that gamblers sing,
and it is a wild song to hear, for the men play a wild
game to-night. Sit where you can see, and watch
these red men play away their belongings, for they are
crazy with the gambler's craze and will not stop until
they have lost all they own."

So then I sat still and watched the game and the
gamblers until Sno-qualm, the moon, made short shadows, and these things I saw there:

A fire had been built to give light for the game, and
on each side of it were six men, who sang a wild chant
and beat with sticks on a hollow drum log.

One man had two short sticks that could be covered by your hand, and all the bark had been peeled
from one, while a ring of green had been left around
the center of the other. These were gamble sticks,
and the game was to guess which hand held the ring
stick. Each side had ten short sticks of cedar, which
lay on the ground in front of them, and besides these
three long sticks had been cut for keeping the count.

When they were ready to play, then one man took
the two gamble sticks, one in each hand, and covered
them so no one could see them, then he swung his

hands crosswise before him, as he knelt there by the fire, and changed the sticks quickly from one hand to the other. Soon one of the other side thought he knew which hand held the ring stick, and he made a motion to that side.

Then the gamble song stopped and the man who held the gamble sticks put both hands out in front, and opened them wide to show both sticks.

The guesser had missed, and so he threw across to the other side one of the short sticks of cedar, which

was one count, and the winners stuck this stick in the ground to show their count of points. Then the game began over, and the gamble chant was sung again

Gamble Sticks.

like this: "A-ah-o-lilly-ahn-ah-ha! A-ah-o-lilly-ahn-ah-ha!"

Then, when one thought he knew which hand held the ring stick again, he made a motion and the sticks were shown as before. This time he guessed it, and so the man who had held the sticks threw a count stick over to the one who had guessed right, and then threw the gamble sticks across too, and his side became the

guessers until they won and got the gamble sticks
back again.

For a long time they did this way, and when one
side had got ten of the count sticks stuck in the ground
they took them all down and put a large one up, to

MADE A MOTION TO THAT SIDE.

mean ten counts, and when one side got three of these
larger count sticks up they won the game and took all
the things that the gamble was for, and left the others
who had lost them.

These things I saw the winners take away with

them: Three canoes, a white man's watch that can tell the time, some good blankets, some pieces of T'kope chicka-min, that the white man, Squintum, calls dollars, and some robes and moccasins, and these were lost by the other side in the play of the sing-gamble.

"You have seen the gamblers and heard their song, T'solo, the wanderer, and now listen:

"These men think to get something for nothing, and that no man may do honestly, and he who does this has in his mind Ka-ke-hete, the chief of demons, and he is evil, or he is pelton, not right in his thoughts, and so is not a good man to know. Remember, T'solo, what you have seen to-night, and do not sit by the sing-gamble fire and listen to the sing-gamble song, lest it bewitch you and you get hungry for gold, like Squintum, the white man, across the mountains, who is never satisfied, and always cries for more gold.

"It is better to know of good hunting, and where many salmon swim, and to have wisdom in the ways of medicine and of magic, than it is to know too much of the ways of Squintum, the white man, who is like the gamblers you saw to-night, in his thoughts."

The fire had burned low and red and I sat there looking into it, and thinking heavy thoughts on the words of the Talking Pine, and as I thought it came

THE FIRE HAD BURNED LOW.   299

into my mind that the Pine was old, and had much
wisdom, and that his words were heavy words, spoken
with a single, straight tongue, so I said, "It is well,
Wise One, and your words are good words to remember, and from this time I will look on the sing-gamble
no more lest I get hungry for the gold, like the white
man, Squintum, and so let Ka-ke-hete come into my
mind. And now I would sleep, and will go to my
lodge. Klook-wah, Wise One."

And so I got in the canoe and crossed back to my
lodge again, and left the fire to burn out.

THE TAH-MAH-NA-WIS OF S'DOAKS

"**W**OULD you know of the Tah-mah-na-wis of S'doaks, T'solo?" asked the Talking Pine, as I lighted my pipe and sat down at his feet to hear the tales.

"Tell the story, Wise One, for I would know of S'doaks and of the tribe of the Twanas," I answered. And then the Wise One, Ka-ki-i-sil-mah, the great Talking Pine, told me this tale:

"When the great medicine man, S'doaks, the son of Yelth, the raven, was only a small lad, he was a good trailer and a good hunter, and was very wise for one so young.

"His eyes were keen and his mind was clear to tell what he saw, and his judgment was the judgment of a man full grown.

302

"Now in the tribe of the Twanas there was an old Mid-win-nie man who was very wise, and who was Itswoot, the bear, and whose nose was keen to smell things out, and this man saw S'doaks and saw his wisdom.

"So one time at the council, Itswoot, the bear, said to Yelth, the father of S'doaks, 'Tyee Yelth, chief of the tribe of the Twanas, you are the favored father of a

S'doaks.

favored son, for S'doaks is of the Mid-win-nie clan, born a medicine man, and only needs to be taught the ways of doing medicine deeds to be a great man and chief of all the Mid-win-nie men. Give to me the training of the lad, and you shall see him the head man of the Twana tribe when the time comes for you to go to Stickeen, the land of the dead.'

"These words were heavy words to Yelth, the raven, and he thought for many days on what the bear had said, and then he told S'doaks that he must go and live with Itswoot, the bear, and get wisdom in the ways of medicine.

"And this was the starting of S'doaks, the greatest medicine man of all the Mid-win-nie clan.

"Now you know, T'solo, the wanderer, that every boy must get a totem, or spirit, to look after him through life and to protect him on his journeys, and to bring luck on his hunting and fishing trips, and this totem is his Tah-mah-na-wis for all time.

"So when S'doaks was a big boy and had seen as many summers as all the fingers on both your hands, and half as many more, then Itswoot called him into the medicine lodge and told him what to do.

"Said the medicine man, Itswoot, the bear, 'S'doaks, listen! To-day you are a man, and must have the totem of a man. Now listen well and I, Itswoot, will tell you of the way. When you leave this lodge you must go to the sweat lodge and stay there without eating or drinking for one whole sun, then when Po-likely, the night, comes, you must leave all your robes, and your bows, and your knife, and with only your medicine belt, go into the forest and stay until your Tah-mah-na-wis comes to you.

"'You must be very careful not to eat or drink during this time, but fast and wait until you see some object that will come to you in the forest and motion for you to follow it. Then you must follow and not take your eyes from it, and it will guide you to food and drink.

S'DOAKS, LISTEN!

" 'This will be your Tah-mah-na-wis and will guard you through life and protect you. In return for this protection you must never kill this object, even if you are starving, but must always protect it in every way you can, for bad luck comes to those who harm their totem.

" 'If your totem be a beast, bird or fish, or other living thing, then get some part of it and put it in your medicine bag for a charm, but do not kill to get this charm.

Knife.

" 'When you have got the charm you may then eat and drink, but let no man see you for one moon, but stay in the forest and talk with Tah-mah-na-wis and gain wisdom.

" 'When the space of one moon has gone by then come here and go again to the sweat lodge and stay over one night, then you may go again among men, and in one summer more you shall take the Kloo-kwallie dance and be a great medicine man. But in that summer, S'doaks, look well that no woman touches you on the hand, and let no woman touch your salmon spear, nor set foot in your fishing canoe, for that would spoil all and make these things useless. And now, S'doaks, have you listened well?'

"'My ears are open and I have heard the roar of the bear,' answered S'doaks.

"'Go then and I will make medicine for your good luck,' said Itswoot, and S'doaks went away.

"All things went as Itswoot had directed, and

I AM TAH-MAH-NA-WIS.

S'doaks was in the forest all alone for many days and had not touched either food or drink, and was weak from long fasting when he heard a voice in a strange tongue, and looking up saw Ki-ki, the blue jay, sitting on the limb of a hemlock tree.

KI-KI TOLD HIM TO REST BY THE RIVER.   309

"Though the language was strange, S'doaks found that he could understand it, as he could the Twana speech of his father's tribe, and then he knew that Ki-ki was sent for him as Tah-mah-na-wis, and he listened to the talk of Ki-ki.

"Said the bird, 'Listen, S'doaks; I am Ki-ki, the blue jay, and I have been looking for you.

" 'I am Tah-mah-na-wis and will show you food and drink. Come, and see that you do not let me get out of your sight.

"So the bird flew from one tree to another, and S'doaks followed until he came to a great river full of salmon, and there the bird told him to stop and rest.

"After S'doaks had rested he said to Ki-ki, 'I, S'doaks, the son of Yelth, the raven, take you for my totem. I must have some part of you for my medicine bag, yet I must not kill to get it. What shall I do?'

" 'Wait,' said Ki-ki, 'and something will happen so you will have the medicine you want.'

"So S'doaks waited, and soon the bird flew away without his seeing it. Then a strange thing happened. As S'doaks sat there, a mink came by dragging a dead blue jay by the neck, and when it saw S'doaks it let go of the bird and ran away into the deep woods.

"S'doaks went and picked up the dead body and took two feathers from each wing and put them in his medicine belt to make him fleet. Then he took the eyes to make him see better, and the heart to make him kind to men, and the brain to make him wise in medicine and to give him the power of Tah-mah-na-wis, and the tongue to give him the talk of the wild things. All these things he put in his medicine belt and sat down to wait for Ki-ki to come back.

"Soon Ki-ki came back and said, 'Now you have the charms and I will go. But I will be near you always, and when you need me you must call in the talk of the blue jay, Ki-ki.'

Mink Dragging a Blue Jay.

"Then Ki-ki went away and S'doaks was left alone. Then he caught some of the salmon and ate them and stayed alone in the woods for the time of one moon and talked with Tah-mah-na-wis and gained wisdom. And so that is how S'doaks, the son of Yelth, the raven, came to have Ki-ki, the blue jay, for his totem.

"Now it is time for sleep," said the Pine, and I got in my canoe again, and paddled away across the Lake of the Mountains to wait.

VOCABULARY AND HISTORICAL APPENDIX.

A-a-ah-na (A-a-ah-nah). — Exclamation from the T'suc-cuc-cub dialect meaning, as nearly as it can be expressed, "Oh yes."

A-ah-o-lilly-ahn-ah-ah.—The chant used in the sing-gamble game. Repeated over and over without time or rythm. Simply these sounds without meaning used as a song to go with the gambling game.

A-he (Ay-hee).—Allied tribes. An exclamation in the T'suc-cuc-cub dialect meaning "yes."

Alki (Al-kee).—Chinook word meaning bye and bye, after a little while, in a little time to come.

Alkicheek (Al-key-cheek).—A small sea shell not unlike a porcupine quill. Considered valuable as ornament among the Indians. Procured from a small mollusk and made into ear pendants, necklaces, etc. Sometimes used as a trade money with Hiaqua in times past.

Canim (Kay-nim).—Chinook word for "canoe."

Cawk (Cawk).—Hiada word. Name of a mythical person described as the daughter of the Beaver.

Chee-chee-watah (Chee-chee-wat-tah).—The name of the humming bird. Allied tribes.

Chee-watum (Chee-wat-tum).—Indian man's name. Allied tribes.

Chethl (Chethl).—A man's name. The lightning. Origin with some tribe of the Selish family.

Chinook.—The name of a group of Indian tribes who lived along the Columbia River, and the sea coast to the north. Also the name of a jargon used as a common trade language among all the Indian tribes of the Northwest who occupy Washington, Oregon, Idaho and Vancouver's Island. It was found, much the same as to-day, in use among these tribes by Lewis and Clark in 1806, and is not, as has been asserted, an invention of the factors of the Hudson's Bay company of fur traders, although they have in company with other traders contributed to its growth by adding English and French words. It is composed as nearly as can be ascertained of the following languages and tribal dialects: French, 90 words; English, 67 words, Canadian, 4 words; Unknown, 24 words; Wasco tribe, 4 words; Chippewa, 1 word; Nisqually, 7 words; Chinook, 221 words; Dialects, 32 words; Chehalis, 32 words; Calapooya, 4 words; Cree, 2 words; Klikatat, 2 words. The English letters F and R are changed to the sounds of P and L and no unnecessary words are used in the jargon, for the Indian favors terseness. Even Chinook has many dialects, and words in common use in one locality are unknown in some distant part of the country where the jargon is used. It has no grammar and a dictionary of it would be hard to write on account of the manifold uses of the same word, a motion accompanying it changing its meaning entirely. Yet it is easily and quickly learned and is in use to a great extent to-day in the Northwest, whites as well as Indians using it as a medium of trade or information. While it has many shortcomings it still has its advantages, and through it the "Totem Tales" have been translated into the English and preserved, a feat that would be almost impossible if one had to rely on the harsh unspeakable gutturals of the native languages, which sound even more confusing than Chinese and each one of which would require half a lifetime to master. The English language is not capable of a description of these Indian tongues. But we have Chinook, only about five or six hundred words, it is true, but it is backed by the expressive talking of an Indian's hands, a natural sign language, and lo, the tales are procured, understood and recorded in all their simplicity, contradictory features, poetry, romance and superstition. So much for the Chinook jargon, a queer language without a country or ownership, a social tramp, an outcast among the languages of the world, just as its originators are outcasts, reviled, laughed at, and misunderstood by the civilized tribes of men who build great stone lodges, all in one place, and seek always for gold, forgetting all, even the Sah-ha-le Tah-mah-na-wis, for this.

Chinoos (Chin-noose).—Tobacco. From the Quinault language.

Closh (Klo-sch).—Chinook word meaning good. Skoo-kum also means good and one word is used as often as the other to signify the same thing.

Colesick (Cole-sick).—The keeper of the dead, chief of all in the country of Stick-een, land of shades. Also used in Chinook to mean any sickness that is not a fever. Origin unknown.

Colesnass (Colesnass).—Chinook word meaning the cold weather, cold wind, etc., etc.

Cultas (Cult-tass).—Chinook word meaning bad, also worthless. "Cultas man," a shiftless fellow; "Cultas esick," a wornout paddle; "delate cultas," very bad, wicked.

Doak-a-batl (Doak-a-battle).—Twana language. The name of a great mythical personage who is credited with the making of many new things. Really an Indian Creator.

D'wampsh (Doo-wam-ish).—The river that empties into Elliott Bay at Seattle, Wash. Name the same as one of the allied tribes whose territory extended many miles up and down this stream.

Ena (E-nah).—Chinook word meaning the Beaver.

Ena-poo (Enah-pooh).—Chinook word meaning Muskrat.

Esick (Ee-sik).—Chinook word for paddle.

Evil Eye.—The expression among Indians meaning about the same as a witch among white people. Anyone possessed of an evil eye is supposed to be able to cast spells for evil over any other person even at great distances. There are many charms and incantations, medicines, etc., etc., to ward off this influence and render it harmless, but notwithstanding all this the Indian is still deathly afraid of the unseen power of this influence, and if he once gets an idea that you are an "evil eye" no power on earth can get him to look at your face, and he will undergo almost anything rather than meet you face to face. Such is the hold of superstition on the savage mind.

G'Klobet (G'Klobet).—Man's name. Allied tribes.

Hah-hah (Ha-ha).—Mythical character. The wife of the frog. Origin unknown.

Hia-qua (Hi-a-quaw).—The name applied to the shells used as money before the whites came among the Indians. The same thing that wampum meant with the Eastern Indians. A word belonging to all of the Selish dialects.

Hiada (Hy-a-dah).—Name of a tribe of Indians who occupy Queen Charlotte's Island, B. C. These are very interesting Indians and are the most advanced of any of the coast tribes. They have many characteristics in common with the Japanese, including the slanting eyes, yellow skin, tracing ancestry through the mother and great love for their children. They are expert workers and carvers in wood and metals and are the canoe and totem pole makers for all the tribes along the coast. Their canoes are the most seaworthy boats afloat for their size, as the writer can attest from experience with them, and the model is almost perfect. They hew these boats from a solid log of Alaska cedar, depending altogether on the eye for measurements and curves, and it is a marvel how they can cut a boat out of the log and have it rest on an even keel, properly balanced without ballast, when put in the water. It is beyond the ken of white men. The great Kuro Siwah, the Japanese current, washes against the shore of their island home and may account for the residence of these North American-Japanese people on this continent by bringing their ancestors here in its drift sometime in the dark ages of the past. Who can tell? They are canoe Indians, and a fish-eating race, and have very many Japanese traits of character, and one is at once struck with the idea that they are degenerated Japanese, and the theory of their origin may be correct.

Hias (Hy-as).—Chinook word meaning a great many, much, large, etc.; "Hias Tyee," a great chief; "Hias hiyu ictas," a very great many things. Hiyu is also used alone in the same sense.

Hoo-ie (Hoo-ee).—Quinault word, meaning crazy.

Hoots (Hoots).—Hiada name for the brown, or cinnamon, bear.

Hootza (Hoot-zay).—Hiada name for the wolf

Hul-loi-mie (Hul-loy-mee).—Quinault language. Meaning different.

Ill-a-hee (Ill-lay-hee).—Chinook word meaning ground or land.

Itswoot (Its-woot).—The Black Bear. Quinault language.

Ka-ke-hete (Kay-kee-hete).—The chief of all demons, origin un-
known, but probably from one of the numerous tribes of the
Selish family occupying the territory along the Columbia
River and north of it along the coast; all being canoe Indians.

Ka-ki-i-sil-mah (Kay-kee-i-sill-mah).—Name of an Indian story
teller of the T'suc-cuc-cub tribe.

Kamas (Kam-mas).—Name of a plant, the roots of which are used
for food.

Ki-ki (Ki-ky).—The Blue Jay. Allied tribes. One of the important
characters in the myths of the Selish tribes. A common totem
or guardian Tah-mah-na-wis with all the coast Indians.

Kit-si-nao (Kit-si-nay-o).—Woman's name from the Hiada language.

Klack-a-mass (Klack-a-mass).—From one of the Selish dialects.
A man's name. Name of a mythic chief.

Kla-how-ya (Klay-how-yah).—The Chinook salutation, "How are
you?"

Kla-klack-hah (Kla-klack-hahn).—A woman's name. Selish dialect. Daughter of Klack-a-mass.

Klale (Klail).—Chinook word meaning any dark color, but usually
used to mean black or dark blue.

Klook-wah (Klook-wah).—Quinault language, west coast of Washington along the Quinault or Quiniault River. Means "good-
bye," or farewell.

Kloo-kwallie (Klue-kwally).—Quinault language. Name given to
the ceremony of the initiation or graduation of a new medicine
man. These rites consist of tortures of various kinds in which
fire plays an important part, and last some times for several
days and always until the candidate for medical honors is
exhausted. These men are sometimes crippled for life by the
horrible tortures inflicted on them by their own hands partly,
and partly by the rest of the dancers. The idea of it all being
to let the medicine man prove himself able to cure his own

hurts before he undertakes to cure others. These rites are gone through with generally several times before the doctor is declared fit for his calling, and are always carried on in the winter season. "Of the Kloo-kwallie" is the best description the author is able to give the reader of the actual ceremony, but cold type cannot bring into the scene the frenzy, the wierdness, and the shivers that chase one another along your spine as you watch these seeming demons dance the Kloo-kwallie. There is a wailing rise and fall to the Indian chant, a subdued fierceness that cannot be described and which can only be heard when they do not know there are listeners about, and this is the song of the Kloo-kwallie, the song that nobody knows and the English tongue does not contain words that will describe it or that will describe the wildness of a ceremony such as the Kloo-kwallie better than it is in "Of the Kloo-kwallie."

Kula-kula (Kull-lah-kull-law).—Chinook word meaning a bird. Used with a prefix thus, Tyee-Kula-kula the eagle, or to translate literally, "the chief bird."

Klutch-man (Klooch-man).—Chinook word, meaning a woman; "Nika Klutchman," my wife; "Hiyu Klutchmen," many women.

Lake of the Mountains.—Lake Union, State of Washington.

Mah-kook (Maw-cook).—Chinook word meaning "trade or barter. Probably the English word "market" adopted and incorporated into the jargon from intercourse with early traders.

Ma-sah-chee (Me-saw-che).—Chinook word meaning the opposite of good. Anything that is worse than just plain "bad."

Medicine bag.—A little bag made of skin usually and containing charms, etc., to ward off evil, sickness, and to bring good luck. The contents are known to the owner, but to no one else, and their potency is immediately lost when any outsider knows what they are composed of. Sometimes the medicine bag is made as a belt and highly ornamented with bead and quill work.

Mem-a-loose (Mem-a-luce).—Chinook word meaning dead. "Cha-co mem-a-loose," to die.

Mid-win-nie (Mid-winny).—The society of medicine men. The ones who practice medicine, magic, religious rites and cast spells. Origin unknown. Common to a great many tribes, but probably of Dakotah origin.

Moos-moos (Moos-moos).—Chinook word meaning elk.

Mowitch (Mow-witch).—Chinook word meaning deer.

Now-itka (Nowitka).—Chinook word meaning yes.

Oke-oke (O-koke).—Chinook word meaning either that or this, according to the way it is used and the motion that accompanies it.

Olo (Olo).—Chinook jargon, meaning hungry.

Opitsah (O-pit-sah).—Chinook word, name of a knife.

Pelton (Pell-ton).—Chinook word meaning crazy.

Pil-Chicamun.—Chinook word for gold. Literally, red metal.

Polikely (Po-like-lie).—Chinook word meaning darkness, night. "Polikely kula-kula," the owl, the night bird.

Puss-puss (Puss-puss).—Chinook word for the cougar or mountain lion.

Quaw-te-aht (Quaw-tee-awht).—Name of a mythic character. Origin unknown other than it belongs to some dialect of the Selish tribes.

Quoots-hoi (Kwoots-hoy).—Name of a mythical witch. Used only in the Thunderbird stories. Selish dialect, but tribe not known. Probably originated with one of the Columbia River tribes who were called Chinook Indians.

Sah-ha-le (Sah-hay-le).—Chinook word meaning up above. Used in connection with Tah-mah-na-wis to mean the Deity.

S'amumpsh (S'mum-psh).—Name of a river in the State of Washington called Sam-mam-ish, by the whites. From the Allied Tribes.

S'doaks (S'ss-doaks).—Hiada language. A man's name.

Shot-o-lil-ie (Shot-o-lily).—Chinook word. Name of the Huckleberry.

Siah (Si-ah).—Chinook word. Far away, a long distance. "Siah Ahncutty," a long time ago; "Siah yowah," away over there.

Siah-ahncutty (Siah-ahn-cutty).—Chinook jargon meaning in the time past. Length of time is indicated by drawing out the

words slightly for a week or so ago, longer for two or three
months, and very long for the time before men can remember.

Siawash (Si-wash).—A name among the whites applied to any Indian of the west coast irrespective of his tribe. Generally
meaning the canoe Indians of Puget Sound and the islands of
the Northwest.

Skall-lal-aye (Skall-lal-a).—Allied tribes. A name for any charm
against the Skall-lal-a-toots or fairy folk.

 Skallalatoot (Skal-lal-a-toot).—A fairy. The unseen and unknown
causes that produce strange noises in the woods. Night voices
of unknown origin. The makers of mischief. Originated with
one of the six tribes who combined under Chief Sealth, or
Seattle as the whites pronounce it. These allied tribes were
the Moxliepush, D'wampsch, Black River, Shillshole, Lake
and T'suc-cuc-cub, the latter being the tribe to which Sealth
properly belonged. Many words contained in "Totem Tales"
are from this group of dialects and are spoken of as the Allied
Tribes when mentioned.

Skamson (Skam-sun).—Hiada language. Name of the Thunderbird. This mythical character is also called Ka-ka-itch, Tu-
tutsh, T'hlu-Kluts and Hah-ness, each being a different tribal
name for the same personage.

Sko-ko-mish (Sko-ko-msh).—Name of a river emptying into Hood's
Canal, Wash.; also name of the Twana tribe of Indians living
on its banks and who belong to the Selish or flathead group or
family of North American aborigines.

Skoolt-ka (Skule-t-kah).—Woman's name from the Hiada language.

Snoqualm (Snow-quallm).—The moon. Originated probably with
the Snoqualmie tribe.

Snugwillimie (Snug-will-li-mie).—Quinault language. Used to
mean friend, but used by an Indian only to mean an Indian
friend, a white friend being either "Tillacum" or "Squintum."

Spe-ow (Spee-ow).—A mythical personage whose deeds as told in
the legends make him occupy the position of a Creator. Legend of Speow and the Spider is very common among the coast
tribes of the Northwest, and can be obtained with slight varia-
tions from a dozen or more different sources.

Spud-te-dock (Spudt-tea-dock).—Twana tribe. A protecting spirit
who was sometimes represented or personified by a wooden
image that was set up in the ground by the medicine man and
by him appealed to for wisdom in deep questions. This is the
nearest approach to an idol that can be traced among the
coast tribes, and while the figure was consulted for knowledge
it can hardly be said that this was done in a religious way,
but more after the form of voo-doo-ism, the conjure work that
is found among all savage tribes. This spirit was merely
made in effigy and this figure consulted and argued with to
give the medicine man knowledge of secrets that he was interested in.

Squintum (Squind-tum).—A white man. Word of unknown origin. Probably from the Allied Tribes, though it may be of
Quinault origin.

Stickeen (Stick-keen).—The country where the dead people live
again. Origin unknown.

Sweat Lodge.—A lodge built for the purpose of taking a sweat or
a steam bath. This is done by heating stones and droppi g
them into a wooden trough containing water until steam is
generated and the one who is taking the bath perspires freely.
It is the Indian turkish bath and is used a great deal in sickness among them.

Tah-mah-na-wis (Taw-maw-na-wiss).—A name applied to anything
the Indians cannot understand. A protecting or guardian
spirit if used another way. Any thing of a magic nature.
Name of the Deity. A Tah-mah-na-wis man is a doctor, priest,
conjurer, and fortune-teller, a dealer in magic and a maker
and destroyer of charms for good and evil, all in the same
personage. "Sah-ha-le Tah-mah-na-wis," the Great Spirit;
"Yah-ka Tah-mah-na-wis," a personal guardian spirit;
"Tah-mah-na-wis ictas," objects of magic or containing
magic properties. "Klale Tah-mah-na-wis," the name of the
secret society of Black Magic. Anything too deep for the grasp
of the Indian mind is charged to "Tah-mah-na-wis," and ends
there, no attempt being made to find out "why."

T'hlingits (Thling-gits).—Name of a tribe of Indians north of Puget Sound. Territory they occupy runs into the Panhandle of Alaska.

Tillacum (Till-lay-cum).—Chinook word for friend.

Tipsu koshoo (Tip-soo ko-sho).—Chinook word meaning water pig, applied to the hair or harbor seal.

T'komah (Ti-ko-ma).—A name from the allied tribes applied to any high snow covered peak. Adopted by the whites and used to mean Mount Ranier, called by some people erroneously as Mt. Tacoma. The Indian name for this mountain means "the one that feeds."

T'kope-mowitch (To-kope-mow-witch).—The Chinook word meaning white goat or white deer.

T'kope (Ti-kope).—White. Chinook word for the color. "T'kope kula-kula," the sea gull.

Too-lux (Tu-lux).—Name of the south wind. Tribal origin not known. Word belongs to some one of the Selish dialects.

Too-muck (Too-muck).—A name applied to all the demons of Indian mythology. Chinook word.

Too-tah (Too-taw).—Name of the thunder. Origin unknown.

Totem (Totem).—A charm against evil.—A protector. This word is found in universal use among all Indian tribes of Central North America and means the same with all. Origin unknown.

Totem Pole.—A carved pole of yellow or Alaska cedar, usually. In no sense an idol. The figures on these poles are symbolic and rarely intended as a portrait of the object represented, though they always have some feature that makes their identity plain, as the ears in the figure for the bear, the teeth in the beaver, the tail in the shark and the whale, the teeth and nose in the wolf, etc. The carvings are family history, tribal history, legendary lore and records of various happenings of a far-reaching character. The carving is done by a few carvers in each tribe, the Hiadas being the most expert and the most lavish in designing. Some of these poles are very large and cost a great deal of time and patience in the manufacture, and are priceless in the estimation of their owners. There are still many things connected with them that are wholly unknown

to the whites and which will likely always remain more or
less of a mystery. Close connection and resemblance has
been found to exist among the carvings of the totem pole, the
monoliths of Yucatan, and the Egyptian stone records, and
some points have even been found in common with the idols
of the Sandwich Islands and the fetishes among the savages of
Africa. All of these things belong more or less to the dark
ages before man kept a record of events, and will go down the
path of time as profound a mystery as when they first dawned
on the horizon of thought and came within the realm of the
scholar. They will always be silent records of a vanished
people.

Touats (Tow-at-ss).—Hiada language. A man's name. The name
of the mythical hunter who figures in the story of the "Hunter
and the Bear."

T'schumin (Ti-schum-min).—The instrument used in making canoes. Name from the allied tribes.

T'set-la-lits (Tee-set-see-lay-litz).—From the T'suc-cuc-cub dialect and first used to designate the first settlement on the
shore of Elliott Bay, Puget Sound, Wash., the site of the pres-
ent city of Seattle.

T'set-shin (Ti-set-shin).—The snake. Origin unknown, but probably from the allied tribes.

T'sing (T'ss-sing).—Hiada word. The name of the beaver.

T'solo (T'ss-solo).—From the allied tribes, meaning lost one, wild,
wanderer.

Tumchuck (Tum-chuck).—Chinook word, meaning falling water.
Applied to any water fall or white rapid in a river. Also name
of a swift mountain stream in State of Washington.

Twana (T-wan-nah).—Name of a tribe of the Selish family of Indians living on the Sko-ko-mish River. Also called Sko-ko-
mish Indians.

Tyee (Tie-ee).—From the Chinook jargon. A chief or head man of
a tribe or family.

T'zum (T'ss-zum). — Chinook word meaning any object that is
painted, printed, written or otherwise marked with color, thus
"T'zum-pish," a spotted fish, the trout; "T'zum-papah," a
printed or written paper; "T'zum-sail," a painted picture,

Wah-wah-hoo (Wah-wah-who).—The frog. Origin unknown, but probably from the Snoqualmie tribe.

Wee-nat-chee (We-natch-chee).—The rainbow. This name originates east of the Cascade range of mountains, but with what particular tribe is unknown. Probably with the Yahkimahs.

* Wee-wye-kee (Wee-why-key).—The Indian name of Princess Angeline, one of the daughters of Chief Sealth and a member of the T'suc-cuc-cub tribe who lived around Elliott Bay, Wash.

Yelth (Yelth).—From the Hiada tribe who live on Queen Charlotte's Island, B. C. The name for the raven, who is one of the mythical characters with this tribe and considered the benefactor of man.

NOTE.—Where the letter T' is followed by the apostrophe, as above, the sound of the T is "tiss," as nearly as it can be written, thus making a syllable of itself, as Tiss-so-low, for T'solo. There are many sounds in the Indian tongues that English has no equivalent for, so they must be represented by the English sound or letter coming nearest.

---

* This character has died since the writing of the above, and leaves many mourners among the early settlers of Puget Sound. She was a noted character and the mascot of the city of Seattle, because in early days she was instrumental in saving the city from Indian massacre. See History of the State of Washington.

www.ingramcontent.com/pod-product-compliance
Lightning Source LLC
Chambersburg PA
CBHW060520030726
47498CB00004B/1009